My Last Remains

by Jill

www.thebookden.com

Library of Congress Cataloging-in Publication Data
ISBN: 0-87714-772-8

ACKNOWLEDGEMENTS

I wish to thank the many people who gave me writing support and/or emotional support for completing this project. Among the many are:

University of Washington professors and faculty:

> Jack Brenner
> Dave Downing
> William Dunlop
> Carole Glickfeld
> Lois Hudson

Dick Gibbons Critique Group
Debbie Chipman / Paula Clayton Critique Group

Fran Beslanwitch
Kim Turner
Kathi Allen
Margaret Ingram
"Gabby"

Chapter 1 - Jacoby

Once or twice a week, right after Dad leaves for work, Mom wants to take me to her friend in the Fisher Building near downtown Detroit. I never want to go there so I hide in the broom closet, behind the couch, under my bed, or wherever I can fit. Mom always finds me and drags me out of the house by my arm.

"No, Mommy," I scream, as she pulls me down the block, toward the bus stop. Sometimes neighbors see me being dragged down the street , but Mom always smiles and says, "She never likes going anywhere."

"No! It's not true!" I yell. I look up at my neighbors with begging eyes and hope they will rescue me. But they ignore me. The men rush off to the factories, as the women, still in their hair rollers, wave good-by or shake their rugs over their porches. And besides, adults believe other adults, not children.

As we pass Mrs. Johnston's house, I see her setting out a bowl of cat food on her porch. She has curly, long brown hair, but in the early morning, it's always wrapped in large pink rollers. She bends down to stroke her cat, then looks over to me when she hears my screams. She nods her head and waves to Mom. My shoes scrape against the sidewalk as Mom pulls my arms and drags me to the bus. I scream as the bus comes and Mom yanks me on.

Mom's friend, Jacoby, has a pediatrics office on an upper floor of the Fisher Building.

Unlike most skyscrapers, it has a theater on the main floor and a fancy lobby with a large gold fish pond. I often wonder if the building is named Fisher because of all those fish.

The elevator door opens and Mom pushes me in. I try to run out, but Mom grabs my arm. The elevator door shuts. "No, Mommy!" I cry. "He hurts me."

She pulls me into his office. In the middle of the waiting room are child-sized chairs around a small table covered with children's books. The waiting room is isolated, sealed off by a door, and no one knows what happens on the other side of that door and down the long hallway where his two examining rooms are. The rooms are opposite each other at the end of the hallway, and where the hallway ends, is a small inner office with a large office desk and a swivel chair.

He puts me in the examining room which has no windows. On the wall is a painting of a basket with a baby in it. You can't see all of the baby, just its arms and legs kicking out of the basket. In one corner of the room is something that looks like an old fashioned hair dryer attached to a metal rod. My mother said it was a kind of lamp. Along one wall is a set of drawers with a baby scale set on top of it. I am trapped in that room while other kids come and go.

I hear his footsteps as he escorts a mother and her little kid from the waiting room through the long hallway and into the other examining room. "Strip him down," he tells the mother. Then I hear the clumping of her high-heeled shoes as he sends her back to the waiting room.

"Children learn independence when their mothers aren't around," he says. The two teen-aged office girls look at each other and laugh.

When he is done, the mother comes to get her crying child.

"Here's a cherry lollipop for little Billy," Jacoby says.

"How nice," I hear the mother say as they leave.

I sit naked on a high examining table in the opposite room. The door is closed just enough so that no one can see me. I want to jump off the table and hide, but I'm afraid of hitting the hard floor, and anyhow, there is no place to hide. My mother sits in Jacoby's swivel chair but strolls back into the room where I am. She looks over to the wall and stares as if in deep thought. She laughs and says, "All those mothers. And they don't know."

Her dark brown eyes stare at the picture on the wall of the baby in the basket. Her short dark brown hair hangs straight, barely covering her ears. Bobby pins keep the front of her hair off her forehead and out of her eyes. She looks almost hypnotized. Then she turns around and leaves to return to the inner office and the swivel chair.

It is there that he keeps his supply of suckers, mainly Tootsie pops. Sometimes he licks the suckers, then rewraps them and puts them back; I watch him sometimes when I go into the inner office with my mother, usually at the end of the day as he gets ready to go home.

He always brings a sack lunch with him. He keeps it in a drawer in his office desk. At lunch time he brings it into the examining room and eats it while I watch.

His two young office girls come back from their lunch break. They point at me and laugh loudly when they see that I am still here. No other kids are here now. They all have mothers who took them home. The afternoon group hasn't yet arrived.

Jacoby closes the door and stands next to me as I sit on his table and he stares at my naked body. I look back at him. He is heavy-set with neatly cut black hair with graying temples. He rubs his fingers up and down the sides of his cheeks as if to admire his clean-shaven face. He stares at me and unzips his pants. He takes out his penis and rubs it against the edge of the table. Then he gets on the table and holds me face down while he pushes his penis into me. He pushes it into my back private.

I can't escape from Jacoby. He holds his needle from his syringe like an ice pick and stabs repeatedly into my buttocks. I scream out for Mom. She doesn't come. I am covered with needle holes. My heart pounds hard against my chest. When he stops to rest, I look at the door. My mind wanders. I think about Diane, the girl down the street from me. We often play together. She has lots of toys so I like playing with her. I have a small rubber rat. Once I held it by its tail and dangled it in front of her. "Look at the rat I found," I said. She screamed.

I turn my head from the door and my eyes hit Jacoby's. His eyes stare at me. He pulls my legs apart and flicks his tongue in and out of his mouth like a snake as he stares. He raises his syringe like an ice pick and stabs. I scream.

I can never forget him. Yet for brief moments while in the torture room, I look at the door and think about my playmates and forget where I am.

His office girl comes into the examining room to announce the arrival of a pharmacy salesman. "Send him back here," Jacoby says in his calm low voice. My mother is wandering about the hallway. Jacoby stops torturing me when his office girl brings the salesman to the doorway.

Jacoby smiles at his guest and invites him into the inner office. There's a strange confused look on the salesman's face. He glares at Jacoby and asks, "Don't you want to finish up with the little girl before we talk?" Jacoby smiles, rubs his fingers along his cheeks and shakes his head no. The salesman looks at Jacoby's smiling face, then he looks at me. Jacoby escorts the salesman out of the doorway and they both disappear into the inner office.

At the end of the day, Mom comes into the room to dress me and take me home. She looks around the room at all the walls, then stares at the baby in the basket, as if she sees something that I can't. She turns to me, "Don't tell anyone what you do here, Jill."

"Why?"

"It doesn't sound nice for you to say anything. Don't tell Daddy."

Chapter 2 - Precursor

My first memory is of the world collapsing. My mother puts me into my baby buggy, a soft padded place of security. Mom gently rocks it back and forth as we wait for my father to join us outside the house. The buggy collapses. My world collapses. I scream. Mom stands there and just stares at me, before she finally lifts me up.

It was the mid 1940's and we lived in a neighborhood where most of the men, including my father, worked in the car factories. After all, we were in the city of Detroit, the motor capital of the world. Women stayed home and cleaned house and took care of children. Divorce was rare and considered to be a disgrace. There were no day care centers.

It was a time when not everyone had refrigerators. Some people used ice boxes. An ice man would come down the streets selling blocks of ice that he kept in an insulated wagon pulled by a couple of horses. Women would run out to the street to buy the ice blocks. Children ran down the street grabbing icicles from the wagon. Licking icicles was a great treat and they were free. In a few years the thrill of chasing the ice man for icicles would be replaced by purchasing ice-cream from ice-cream men in motorized trucks.

Some of the houses on our street were single homes and some were two flats. We lived in a two flat during my early years. An elderly but attractive deaf woman with a long French braid lived in the upstairs unit and we lived downstairs in a three bedroom unit. I had one bedroom, my older brother Maurie, who was 8 years older than I, had a bedroom, and my parents shared the third one.

I never knew anything about that old woman upstairs. We lived in the same building separated by walls. I knew nothing of her and she knew nothing of me. She spent all her time in her house, I can't imagine doing what. She couldn't hear a radio, and not many people owned televisions. T.V. was a new Invention. It was a wooden box with a 7" screen that displayed black and white moving pictures. Just what that old woman did all day, I'll never know. She never spoke to anyone. She never heard anyone.

She never heard my screams from my crib the day my mother walked out on me. Dad had left for work and Maurie left for school. Mom tossed out all the baby food and milk and left. It was my fate that the nearest person to me was deaf. They found my mother several days later in New York. She had gone to visit her cousin.

Mom was the youngest of seven children. Her family had come to the U.S. from Rumania, but she was born here. When Dad met her, she was a teen-ager who had dropped out of high school. Her sisters and brothers were married and no longer lived at home. Her parents rented out the empty rooms. Mom was not well liked among her peers. Her behavior did not mesh with what was expected of a young girl in the early 1900's. She was known to run around the house and yard in only her underwear. She had no interest in working or finishing school.

Dad grew up in Poland and hardly spoke English. His mother was only in her twenties when she died and left four young children. Grandpa had a bad temper and wasn't much of a father for his kids. He remarried to a woman who my father liked. When the marriage didn't work out, Dad lost a second mother. Grandpa married again and had two more children with the third wife. The four older children were jealous of the two new siblings because the younger kids had a mother. It was a difficult time inside and outside the family. Nazis were coming into power, and my grandfather knew he'd have to get his wife and two sets of children out of Poland. My father was left in Poland with his five fighting siblings and his stepmother while Dad's father came to

America hoping to earn enough money to send for the rest of the family. Not an easy feat for a man who could not speak English. He became a junk peddler. He was just about to send for Dad's two oldest siblings who were by now in their early teens. Grandpa figured they could find work and help to save to get the others here. But, word came that his third wife had died and Grandpa had to rush back to Poland.

He later returned to the U.S. and started over. This time, as he was about to send for the two oldest children, the U.S. closed its door to more immigrants. Grandpa managed to get the two older kids into Canada where they lived with some cousins who were able to get there. Later on my father and his sister came to Canada. Grandpa stayed in Detroit and struggled to save money to bring over his two youngest children. Eventually, my father and the other three teen-agers were allowed into the U.S. The two younger ones arrived from Poland. They lived on the same block where Mom and her family lived. When Mom met Dad, she followed him to work each day and spent the day in his car waiting for him. She would invite him over to her house where my grandmother always offered him something to eat. My Dad told everyone that he wanted to marry Mom so he could have her mother as his own. So Mom and Dad were married.

My parents often reminded me of praying mantises. Those large insects, that during the mating act, the female kills her mate. That's how Mom and Dad seemed to me. Dad was emotionally crippled with feelings of helplessness. He was a little boy who spent his life trying to find a mother. And Mom, the female praying mantis, abused him. He could not leave her because he saw himself as a child who could not leave his mother. This is the world into which I was born.

Chapter 3 - The Doll

It was Saturday. I woke up and screamed. Another nightmare. No one knew why I was forever having nightmares. I dreamt my mother turned into a monster and tried to kill me. People in my dreams were tortured and burned alive. I saw dead babies in baskets.

My screams woke my parents. Dad shrugged it off, saying that all children have nightmares.

Dad had to work that day. He often worked on Saturday. Maurie went out somewhere playing with his friends. I hardly saw that big brother of mine. When he wasn't in school, he was outside riding his bike, or playing with other boys his age. He was a teenager and I was four. Mom had some shopping to do downtown. She was fat and ready to have a baby. I was excited because I wanted someone I could play with.

I liked shopping downtown with Mom because we always stopped at the toy department in Hudson's Department Store. It was a jungle of toys. On that particular Saturday, Mom let me pick out a blond doll with blue eyes and long eye lashes. She wore a red and white striped dress with red and white bows in her yellow hair. Her shoes were white, with red and white laces. And she had a cute smile on her face with tiny dimples on her cheeks. I carried her around in my arms as we followed Mom around the store. By the time we got home I was tired and fell asleep with my doll.

On Sunday, as on most Sundays, Dad made breakfast. He took a carton of cottage cheese and a carton of sour cream and mixed them together with boiled potatoes and chopped cucumber. He called it a farmer's salad.

I sat down and ate with my new doll. I kissed her on her nose, and she smiled.

Dad walked over to the stairway and yelled, "Maurie! Come eat!"

Only silence from Maurie. Dad came back to the kitchen where he and Mom ate, then both left the room. I was still munching away when Maurie finally came. He sat down, grabbed his fork, and ate.

"Hi," I said.

"You just behave yourself and don't bother Mom!" he answered.

I don't know why he thought that I might bother her. Dad came back into the room. "You kids got enough to eat?"

"Yeah," we both answered.

Maurie looked up at Dad. "I need a dollar, Dad."

"What do you need to waste a dollar on!" he yelled as he searched his pocket for money. He handed Maurie 4 quarters and continued to complain. "No one ever gave me nothing! I had to work for everything! I didn't even have a mother. It wasn't easy coming here from Poland. No mother."

I looked up at Dad. He was chubby and sad. Those were his two main characteristics. He was an overweight little kid, always hungry and always complaining about his life. His limited English made him even more childlike.

Maurie quickly swallowed the last of his food, wiped his mouth with the back of his hand and walked out of the house. That was all that I saw of Maurie the rest of the day. He was only in the house when he was eating or doing homework, and either way he was too busy to say very much.

Dad continued talking to no one about how he never got anything from anyone, and how he lost his home to the Nazis. I munched on cucumbers. I liked the crunch. It was like eating potato chips. My doll looked at me, and I winked at her.

In the afternoon, Mom's cousin Sylvia came over with her husband Simon and their daughter Dee who was my age. Both of us would be 5 soon and starting kindergarten in the fall. It was rare for us to get company. The adults sat down in

the living room and talked, but Dee and I preferred to play
with jacks. I never could understand how adults could just sit
and do nothing but talk. They looked like a bunch of tired
bears about to hibernate. They were sprawled out over the
heavy bulky stuffed chairs with Mom dominating the couch
as usual. Sylvia was short and thin and rather fragile looking
with a long thin nose. Her husband was short too, but he was
a fat bear.

"Go show Dee your new doll," Mom said, as she turned
her head away from the bears and toward me.

"But we're in the middle of a game," I answered.

"Do it anyway!" she snapped.

I went to my room and brought out my doll. I held her
snugly in my arms and kissed her cheek as she looked at me,
and everyone watched. Dee got up off the floor, and walked
over to her mother. She pointed to the doll and started crying.
"I want the doll," she said. Her parents laughed.

My mother pulled the doll from my arms and handed it to
Dee. "Here'" she said with a big smile on her face. "Keep it.
I'm going shopping again tomorrow and I'll buy another doll
for Jill."

I looked up at Dee's parents. Both of her parents were
smiling at her and her new doll. Her mother hugged Dee. I
looked up at Dad hoping he would protect me. But he was
also looking at Dee, and smiling None of the adults cared
about the tears in my eyes. I went to my room and sat on my
bed while Dee played with my doll. I heard the adults laugh.
I listened while they left.

"Dinner's ready," Dad called out to me after a while.

"No," I answered and remained in my room the rest of the
day.

The next morning, I heard Dad leave for work. I lay on my
bed already dressed because I hadn't put on my pajamas from
the night before. A little later, I heard the front door slam. It

was a Maurie slam. He left for school. Maurie was tall and thin and didn't look strong enough to make the door slam with such thunder. He must have come home late in the evening because I didn't even hear him. I must have fallen asleep.

I was hungry and finally left my room to go to the kitchen. Mom was there drinking coffee. She wore a house dress, fuzzy house-slippers and lots of bobby pins in her hair.

"Mom, are we going shopping now for another doll?"

"No!" she answered. "One doll is enough for you. I'm not buying another one."

I grabbed some bread from the kitchen table and went back to my room. I sat on my bed and held my pillow. Some tears fell on it . I thought about Dad. Maybe he would help me. But there was no way to talk to him until he came home and that wouldn't be till evening. I waited in my room. I was acting like adults, just lying around doing nothing. I wiped my face in my pillow and bounced up and down on my bed. I walked around in circles in my room like a caged prisoner.

When Dad finally came home, I ran out of my cage and to the front door to meet him. I swung my arms around him and grabbed on to his pant legs. "Mom won't buy me my doll!" I sobbed. "She gave my baby away."

Dad looked at me sadly and watched my tears. He turned to Mom who was lying on the couch. Her house dress was wrinkled, her hair still full of bobby pins. She hadn't changed clothes or combed her hair all day.

"Maybe you should buy her another doll," he said.

"No!" Mom yelled.

Dad shrugged his shoulders and looked down at the floor. I looked at his face. It was a sad face. "We can't argue with Mom," he said. "There's nothing we can do."

Chapter 4 - Johnny

Mom had to go to the hospital to have our new baby. Dad took me to Mom's oldest sister. Mom's six siblings were far apart in age. Mom was the youngest and her sister Belle was old enough to be my grandmother. I never knew my grandmother because she died before I was born. Grandpa was still alive, though, and approaching 90.

Whenever Mom went to the hospital, I was taken to Aunt Belle. I hated her, but was sent there a lot because Mom was often put into the hospital. She had some kind of "nervous disorder" that no one ever explained to me.

In front of Dad, Aunt Belle acted nice, but as soon as he left and I was alone with her, things changed. She looked at me and her tongue slid across her bright lipstick-covered lips. She gazed at me like a hungry animal about to attack easy prey. I looked at her tongue, then at her white hair. She didn't wear bobby pins like Mom. Aunt Belle went to the beauty shop a lot. Her hair had waves and every strand knew where it was supposed to go. I looked at the walls. All the walls in her house were painted white and everything looked very clean. Her tongue gave a hungry flick.

I could hear Uncle Al, getting ready to go to work. He flushed the toilet then gargled with mouth wash. He was always concerned about having good breath and making good impressions on customers at the small furniture store that he ran. He came out of the downstairs bathroom and walked toward the front door straightening his tie.

As he was about to leave, Aunt Belle turned to him. "My mother used to make me take care of my sister! Now I'm supposed to take care of her damn kid!"

Uncle Al stopped at the door and put his hands on his waist. He was a skinny little guy. He looked so small next to Aunt Belle.

"Belle!" he said. "If you don't want to do it, just send her back."

"No." Belle puffed as she turned her head back toward me. Her eyes glued themselves to me, and her pale pink tongue licked more lipstick off her lips. "I'll get even."

Uncle Al turned around and left. I wanted to run out of the house with him and hide somewhere, but Aunt Belle grabbed my arm and dragged me upstairs. I tried to hang on to the hand rail along the stairway, but she pulled hard and I was dragged up the stairs.

"I'm going to make you, Sister!"

"I'm not your sister!" I screamed. She pulled me into the bathroom and locked the door. She grabbed her douche bag, and filled it up with water. I tried to pull away. She pulled my pants down, and stuck it up my back private.

"My insides will burst!," I screamed. She licked some lipstick off her lips.

*

Finally Mom came home with our new baby and I was able to leave Aunt Belle. I was excited when Dad came to pick me up and rescue me. I stuck my tongue out at Aunt Belle and ran to Dad's car.

I was so happy to be home and see our new baby. The first thing I wanted to do was hold him. He was a cute baby. His skin was darker than mine. In fact, I looked pale next to him. And he had beautiful curly black hair. My hair was straight like Mom's. My new baby didn't look like me, but he didn't look like anyone else in the family either. I was proud of my new brother.

Johnny would have to sleep in a crib in Mom's and Dad's room, and later he could share Maurie's room. I sat on Mom's bed across from the crib, and Mom let me hold Johnny in my arms. He opened his eyes. He hadn't done that when Mom was holding him. I think he knew that we were going to be good friends.

Our house became a busy place because several relatives and neighbors stopped by to congratulate Mom and Dad. I felt excited and happy, but Maurie didn't seem very happy about having another kid in the house. Mom's dad and his brother Uncle Frank came too. They were both small, wrinkled-up men, and Uncle Frank walked with a cane. They both smoked cigars, and I liked to wear the paper rings that came on each cigar. Whenever they came to our house, they brought me presents. The two men sat stiff and silent as they stared at Mom and Dad showing Johnny off to a couple neighbors. Maurie and I sat on the living room floor playing with some spinning tops that Grandpa and Uncle Frank brought me. Grandpa was as still and silent as the chair he sat on. His grim expression looked as if it had been starched on.

Uncle Frank tapped his cane. "You stick to your older brother, Jill," he said. "Someday, your younger brother will grow up and move away."

I looked up at Uncle Frank. His face looked tired. I didn't understand why he said that. I looked at Maurie. He turned his head to the floor, as if he had just been yelled at. Mom and Dad looked proud as Mom held our new baby.

"He's so cute," I broadcasted. I picked up my tumbled tops and continued to spin them on the floor. I was happy.

Chapter 5 - Kindergarten

I started kindergarten and had to leave my new baby home alone with Mom. Sometimes she left us home by ourselves. That was O.K. because I crawled into his crib and played with him so he wouldn't cry. But now I worried about him being alone without me. I worried about how Mom treated him when he was alone with her

A couple weeks into the semester, I caught a terrible cold but was sent to school anyway. My nose dripped all over. I picked up my dress and blew.

"Jill!" my teacher screamed. "Don't use your dress!"

I lifted my head up so I could see my teacher's face. I felt like a mouse looking up at a giraffe. She was tall and chunky. Her large round eye glasses made her eyes look like large round beach balls. I smiled at her. Her face was angry.

"What do you want me to use?" I asked. "Mommy told me to use my dress."

"Get into the corner! You can just stand there all day!"

"Why?" I asked.

"For lying about your mother!"

"But, I'm not lying," I insisted.

The teacher grabbed my arm and pulled me to the corner. "Face the wall!" she yelled I turned around to ask another girl if she knew what I was supposed to do. The teacher pushed me back into the corner and told me not to talk to anyone. I couldn't wait till I could go home and ask Mom for help.

As soon as I reached home, I told Mom that I was forced to stand in the corner all day because the teacher didn't want me to use my dress to wipe my nose. I asked Mom if she would ask my teacher what I was supposed to do.

"No." Mom said. "If your teacher doesn't want you to use your dress, then use your slip."

The next day I used my slip, but the teacher was angry

again. I smiled nicely at her and politely explained, "I'm doing what Mom told me to do. Call her and ask her."

My teacher exploded in anger, dragged me into the corner and made me stand there again all day facing the wall.

Stunned and confused, I turned my head and whispered to a boy in my class asking if he knew what I should do. "I don't know," he said. "My Mom won't let me go to school with a cold."

"Face the wall and don't talk, Jill!" the teacher screamed at me.

Dad was my only hope. The minute he walked into the house from the factory, I ran to him and blurted out what happened. In his sweatshirt and heavy slacks he looked just like the boys in my class, except that Dad was bigger.

"I don't know what to do," he said. "Go ask Mom. That's what she's for. She needs to do something around here. She hardly even cooks for me."

"But Mom doesn't know!" I insisted.

"Go ask Mom," he said again.

"Dad. I need you to call my teacher for me. Maybe she'll tell you what I'm supposed to do. She doesn't like when I use my dress, and kids aren't allowed to run in and out of the bathroom. So I don't dare make her even more mad by going in and out for toilet paper!"

"My English is no good, Jill. Ask Mom to help you."

Everyday at school, I stood alone in the corner until my cold was over.

First grade wasn't much better. At the beginning of the semester, we were given coloring books. Our teacher said we could take them home for the weekend to show off to our friends, but we had to remember to bring them back the following Monday. During the weekend, I colored all of the pictures, and as the teacher requested, I brought it back on

Monday. The teacher decided to start off our day by having us open the coloring book to the page where the clown was. She told us to color the hat yellow and his suit brown. Mine was already colored in blue and orange, and I put bright red on his buttons. I thought those colors were much better for a clown. The teacher walked around the room to see how we were coloring. I tried to scrape off the blue with my finger nail and color over my blue and orange and red, with yellow and brown, but it didn't work very well. When the teacher saw my coloring, she looked at me as if she wanted to hit me. Her eyes squinted and she put her hands on her hips and yelled, "You don't know how to follow directions! Those are not the colors I told you to use!"

I sat there and forced a smile at her. I didn't say one word. I was afraid that if I explained that the pictures had already been colored, she would be even more angry. That's the way it had been in kindergarten. Whenever I tried to explain anything to my kindergarten teacher, she thought I was lying and I would have to stand in the corner all day. So, now, in first grade, and for much of my life to come, I was unable to defend myself. The teacher's words were painful as they echoed through my ears, "Jill! You don't know how to follow directions!"

All of grade school was painful. Girls had to wear dresses even in cold weather. We weren't allowed to wear warm slacks like the boys. And any kid who wanted to use the restroom had to raise his hand and announce the intention to the whole class and beg permission. Needing to pee is a very personal matter, and I wasn't about to raise my hand and in front of everyone say what it was I needed to do. One time in first grade, I vibrated in my chair trying to hold it in. But finally I sprung a leak and pee poured from my chair. None of the other kids noticed. But the teacher happened to walk by. "What is the water under Jill's chair?" she asked.

"I don't know," I answered. I looked up at the ceiling as if to be looking for a leak.

She glared at me in anger, "You don't know how to do anything right! You don't pay attention." She called in the janitor and ignored me for the rest of the day.

*

My baby brother was getting bigger. We were moving to a bigger house. Mom and Dad found a two-story, single-family home. Johnny would now have his own room, and by the time Johnny enters kindergarten, Maurie will have graduated from high school and have moved away.

Chapter 6 - Anointment

I knew the footsteps coming to my door were Johnny's. His footsteps were those of a giant. For such a small boy he sure was loud. I quickly grabbed my pillows and stuffed them under my blanket, then ran into my closet.

"Jill. Wake up. Time to play," he yelled as he entered my room. "It's Saturday, you know. No school today"

I watched Johnny through my closet key hole. He pounced on my pillows, trying to wake them up. I pulled my sock off my right foot and stuffed it in my mouth so he wouldn't hear my giggling.

"Aha! So you're in the closet. I knew you were in there all along."

"Oh? Then how come you pounced on my pillows?"

"Well, um, I left something downstairs, Jill. Hurry and get ready so we can play." Then he ran out my door.

A few minutes later his giant footsteps approached my door again.

"Jill, you ready?"

"Sure, come on in."

There was another lump in my bed.

"O.K. Jill, I know you're in the closet."

Right to the closet the small giant ran, and there went the pillows, from the top of the closet right on his head. I was giggling. In spite of a mouthful of sock, I couldn't control my giggling. The lump in my bed giggled like a chimpanzee.

"I'll fix you, Jill."

He was now beating up the giggling lump with a pillow. The giant was beating up on the chimp.

"What's all that noise up there?"

"Oh, nothing, Mom." he called out. I was being clobbered to death with pillows and Johnny said it's nothing.

"Well, if the two of you have nothing better to do, you can come down here and help me."

"Yeah, pretty soon, Mom," said Johnny as he kept pounding away at the wiggling lump.

"Oh, come on, Johnny. You're hurting my pillow!"

"No, I don't think your pillow hurts."

"Well, maybe we should see what Mom wants."

"No, this is more fun."

"I'll make breakfast for you, if you stop hurting my pillow."

We went downstairs and into the living room. "Pistachio nuts!" he yelled as he grabbed a giant handful and started cracking the shells. I grabbed an even bigger bunch.

"You'd better stop eating these all up or Mom will get mad," I told him, as I continued to munch.

"It's too late, Jill. Look how much we've eaten."

"I've got an idea," and I ran upstairs, grabbed my glue, and ran back down.

"What are you gonna do with the glue?"

"See Johnny, we'll just glue the shells back together and no one will know the difference."

"Will you two get in here and help me! I need help finding my furniture polish. I've looked everywhere and can't find it. I'm going to shine up all my silverware today."

"With furniture polish?" Johnny said.

"Shh....Johnny, don't question Mom."

Johnny wrinkled up his face, and his eyes looked at me as if he were waiting for me to tell him some secret.

"I'm sick of you lazy brats. Now come into the kitchen and help me!"

The three of us looked through the cabinets and closets. I finally found the polish behind the aspirin bottle in the medicine cabinet, and Johnny and I ran outside to play.

When I came back into the house, Mom was lying on the couch. She was always lying on the couch. She looked up at me as I entered the living room.

"Oh, it's depressing being a married woman! I can't wait till you're married, Jill. Then it will be your turn. The worst thing that happens in life is when you're an adult and there's nothing in life left to do but marry. It's a last resort! The last thing before death."

I just stood there and wanted to cry. I don't want to grow up, I thought to myself. Can't climb trees or play hide and seek anymore, if you're a grownup. No one buys you toys anymore. No one wants you living at home anymore. It's just like being dead. I don't want to ever grow up. I don't want to get older, then older, and DIE for always.

"You brat! Why are you standing there staring at the floor! When are you going to grow up! I can't wait till the day you move out of this house!"

I wished Mom loved me and didn't want to get rid of me. It's hard trying to be like other kids when you have a mother who doesn't love you. Everybody wonders what's wrong with me that even my own mother doesn't love me.

I stood there thinking and didn't move. I looked at the rug under my feet and for a moment felt like a stone statue. Johnny ran into the house. Pigmy giant footsteps were running into the living room.

"Mom! Larry Jones and his brother pushed me off my bike and I got a scraped knee!"

Mother's voice pounded into my ears as she yelled at Johnny. "Good! You should be pushed off the earth. You're a freak! I WISH YOU'D DIE!"

She picked up her water glass, and as hard as she could, she threw it at Johnny. He jumped back, and stared at the tiny icy pieces of glass that smashed in front of him.

"It's O.K.," I said as I pulled him by the arm. "Let's go outside by the water faucet."

He was heavy to pull. His body was stuck.

"It's O.K., Johnny. Mom didn't mean it. She always talks that way. It's her nerves acting bad. You know she has bad nerves. That's how come she goes to the hospital sometimes. Please talk. Here, let me rinse your knee off under the water faucet. Please Johnny, look at me."

We stayed outside, but after awhile we both got pretty hungry. My pigmy giant brother and I both had giant appetites.

"Jill, I'm getting hungry. Think we can go in for dinner?"

"Sure, Johnny. Dad is probably home from work now and dinner is probably ready."

"What if Dad didn't come home again?"

"Well, if he didn't, and if Mom is still resting on the couch, we'll cook our own dinner. I'll make some chocolate peanut butter soup."

"Jill, I don't see Dad's car around."

"Wait here. I'll go first."

I sneaked in through the back door, looked around the kitchen, then ran back out.

"It's O.K., Johnny. Mom made stew for us."

Johnny and I raided the stew pot. Mom was resting on the couch and didn't seem to notice us.

*

Monday morning, I woke up and ran into Johnny's room. "C'mon, Johnny, we got to go to school now. Hurry and keep quiet so you don't wake Mom. I'll go fix breakfast."

I dressed quickly. I only buttoned some of the buttons on my dress, then ran downstairs and cooked oatmeal. I dumped a big gob of it into Johnny's bowl, then put a handful of raisins on top of it. His cereal looked as if it had measles.

I started scraping out the cereal pot and wondered why it was taking Johnny so long to get downstairs. I hoped he could get himself down to the kitchen without waking Mom.

I continued scraping the pot. I burned it again. Finally I heard him coming. It's about time, I thought. I glanced over as he sat down to the table. He picked up one of the raisins from his cereal and held it between two of his fingers. He looked at it as if it were a bug. I stood by the sink and continued to scrape out the pot. Mom's pots always burned. I just knew it was because those pots weren't made right.

"Hey, Johnny. What happened to my juice?"

I looked at him and we both giggled. The pigmy and the chimpanzee couldn't stop their giggling. I knew what he did. He scooped up a giant handful of his raisined cereal and dumped it in my bowl. Then he drank up his juice, and switched his empty glass with mine.

"Look Johnny! Look at that on the floor."

He looked down and I grabbed a handful of cereal and put it right back in his bowl.

"There's nothing down here."

He looked up at me and at his cereal. He giggled when he saw how much it had grown.

"Yipe!" he screeched, " I just remembered I'm supposed to be in school early today, and help Mrs. Wadds with the movie machine."

He poured his glass of milk down his throat. "Oh, here's something for you, Sis."

"What is it? Come on. Open your hand so I can see."

I pried open his hand while he stood there and laughed at me. It was a raisin.

"See you later," he said, and he ran out the door, still laughing at me.

I felt a sense of relief. It was my chance to sit and rest. With him off to school I didn't have to worry about his waking Mom. I liked sitting at the kitchen table. It was all by itself in a little nook, just off the side of the kitchen. The wallpaper had pictures of Dutch children with windmills. The Dutch children wore bright red pants and bright yellow wooden shoes. Their shirts were yellow too, with a little red button on each pocket. I loved those little Dutch children. They were my friends. All of them watched me.

I heard the sound of house-slippered feet sliding along the floor. Darn it! Mom would have to wake up now.

"Hi, Mom."

She looked right at me but acted as if she didn't see me. She looked as if she were daydreaming. I sat at the table and wished she'd comb her hair and look pretty like other moms. Her hair was ear length and hung straight like pins. The top of her head was full of bobby pins. She had more of those pins on her head than hairs. She was carrying her candelabra. It was heavy, and she held it tightly, chest high with both hands. "I'm anointing today," she said.

I sat there and finished buttoning my dress.

"I spent a lot of time preparing for this. I polished all my silver."

"Yes, Mom, I know."

"I'm anointing today." She stepped toward me. "I'm in power now. My candelabra will CRUSH your skull until you're anointed."

I stood up. *She doesn't know what she's doing! Her nerves are--sick again.*

"You'll be anointed today, Grape. You and that little grape you are always protecting and hiding. You can't hide from me now."

There's no door in the nook! No windows! No one around!

"You can't hide this time."

She's between me and the only door! I stepped back. The wall pushed me.

"This time I am the anointing judge."

I'll smile, I won't be scared. She's moving closer!

"You grape, once and for all, will be anointed."

When she's like this I grab Johnny and run. I can't run this time. The wall pushes me.

"You, Grape, finally, your turn."

She's moving closer!

"Grapes were made for crushing."

Johnny. what will you do when you come home? Don't look at my face, Johnny.

"Wine will flow from you, Grape."

The candelabra - It's over my head. Johnny. Don't look at me.

"Wine will fill my rivers."

Johnny. Don't try to wake me.

"Wine. Flowing wine."

Mother's eyes. Staring at me.

"I'll have my wine."

Johnny, I couldn't run this time.

"Anointment Day, Grape."

I won't be hiding in the closet, Johnny. Pillows won't fall. There's no lump in my bed. Not this time. Johnny.

"Red wine from Grape."

I won't giggle, Johnny. Don't try to wake the lump. You were fun Johnny.

You pounded away with a pillow at the wiggling lump. Johnny, you can't wake

She stumbled.

I pushed ...hard.

Those Dutch children... ......crushed ... into the wall.

I ran.

Chapter 7 - The Relatives

I ran out of the house and went to school as if nothing had happened. I didn't know of anyone who might help. Dad had no power over Mom. It wasn't going to help to tell him. And whenever I told Maurie anything, he would yell at me for bothering his mother. Johnny and I would just have to be careful till Mom got into a better mood or someone took her to a hospital.

Mom had become an over-charged battery. For several days she danced about the house non-stop. She sang can-can music and up went her legs in rhythm to her music. She acted like a chorus girl.

I waited on the school yard for Johnny to get out of his class so we could walk home. He staggered out like a drunk from a bar.

"What happened, Johnny?"

He didn't say anything. I could tell from the way he walked that his leg hurt.

"What happened?" I asked again.

"The kids pushed me down at recess and called me names," he finally mumbled. We walked home and went into the garage to wait a couple hours for Dad to come home.

"Hi," he announced when he saw us. "Let's go in and eat."

We followed him into the house and into the kitchen. Dad looked at the stove. There wasn't any food cooking, and we could hear Mom upstairs singing can-can music.

"Look how she treats me!" Dad complained. "She's having a good time all day while I work hard for her in the factory, and she doesn't even cook for me!"

He stood looking at the empty stove. I didn't say anything. Mom came dancing down the stairs singing. She was nude.

"Why don't you cook something?" He pouted.

Up went Mom's leg as she sang.

Dad's eyes were crying, and his nose sniffed. "I work so hard for her and all she does is play."

Mom grabbed an empty pot and beat it like a drum. She kicked her leg up, then threw the pot at Dad. Her eyes stared out as if she were on a stage and looking out towards her audience.

"Dad, maybe you should take her to the hospital again," I said.

"There's nothing wrong with Mom," he snapped. "She just likes to play!"

She picked up a spoon and threw it at his head. Dad went over to the couch and cried. "She doesn't want to cook for me," he sobbed. "She doesn't care if I eat or not. O.K. for her, I won't eat if she won't feed me, I'll just die. She'll be sorry."

"I hate her, Dad. She's crazy."

"She's not crazy, Jill! She just doesn't love me." He pressed his lips together.

"I never had anyone who cared about me," Dad continued. "My dad hated us kids. He used to beat us with his belt whenever he was upset about something. Even though it had nothing to do with us kids."

Dad used the palm of his hand to wipe some tears off his cheeks and continued on.

"I still have marks on my back from my Dad beating me. And I lost my mother when I was a baby." Dad's tears soaked his shirt. "All I ever wanted was someone to care about me. I've been so good to Mom. No one ever loves you like your real mother, and I lost mine. All I ever wanted to do was get married so I could have someone care. But it doesn't work."

I looked at Dad and my throat felt stiff. I wished his mother wouldn't have died. I wondered what would have happened if it would have been my mother that died instead.

I wondered if I would have been like Dad, wishing that she wouldn't have.

"Maybe someone in your factory can help us," I said.

"You know I don't have any friends, Jill. How can I have any friends when Mom always acts up?"

Johnny walked past Dad and me and went upstairs. My body felt heavy as I sat on the couch with Dad. I wanted to get up and go upstairs to see what Johnny was doing. My body wouldn't move. We could hear dishes being smashed on the floor as Mom danced and sang the can-can.

"Dad, call a doctor!"

"It won't do no good," he said. "They'll just take her away and when she comes back she'll be mad at me. It never does no good."

More dishes smashed in the kitchen, and I thought about Johnny upstairs. Dad cried. Through the tears and sniffles, he mumbled about how he escaped from Poland because the Nazis were there. He continued talking. "I thought she loved me. I came to this country when I was 16. She lived on our block." He blew his nose. "She dropped out of high school, and she followed me to work everyday and got into the back seat of my car and waited there all day till I finished work. She was the only one who didn't make fun of me and call me greenhorn."

Mom entered the room and up went her leg, kicking Dad in the head. Then she danced her way back into the kitchen. I didn't want to leave Dad by himself, but I was worried about Johnny upstairs. I stood up.

Dad held his head where Mom had kicked him. "Someday I'll leave her. She'll be sorry." He stood up and continued, "I'll call her sisters and brother."

"No, call your brothers and sisters."

He went to the phone and dialed. "No, I want her family to come. I'll call Maurie too," he said.

I always hated her family. They weren't much better than her older sister Belle. She, like Mom, lived in a sleep-walking dream and she couldn't be awakened. We were hungry but Aunt Belle wouldn't give us food. We were toys. Toys don't need to be fed.

I remember a time when Johnny had to stay at Belle's house but I stayed home with Maurie and Dad, because I was in school and Johnny was still a preschooler. When Johnny finally came home, he couldn't speak for several months.

Mom's sister Rebecca was nicer, though also crazy, and in and out of mental hospitals. She tried to kill one of her kids once. Yet, I remember going shopping with her and she bought me new clothes. The insane are inconsistent. Even Mom sometimes would come home from the hospital and bake chocolate brownies for me. It seemed as if they were all sleepwalkers, living out bizarre dreams.

I wished Dad would call his family instead of Mom 's. They always told him to get a divorce and take us kids with him. That's what I wanted him to do. But he had stopped calling his family years ago. They didn't even visit us anymore.

And Maurie never helped. Maurie always acted like he didn't like having a brother and sister. And he never wanted any of his friends to know about Johnny. I loved Maurie, but I hated him. He used to be helpful to have around. When I had that terrible cold in kindergarten and kept getting in trouble for blowing my nose in my dress the way Mom taught me, it was Maurie who finally told me that instead of my dress or raising my hand and waiting for permission to go to the lavatory, I should just TELL the teacher that I need toilet paper and go! Dad never gave me information. He'd tell me not to bother him. He would come home from work hungry. His fat stomach never seemed to get enough. "Don't ask me questions," he'd say. "I'm hungry."

"Maurie is here," Dad yelled out from downstairs.

"Coming."

I went downstairs. Maurie was all dressed up, like he just came from work. Dad sat on the couch with tears leaking from his eyes, and Maurie stood there yelling at Dad. It was as if Maurie was the father and Dad was his little boy being scolded.

"I'm sick of you always calling me," he yelled at Dad. "You mess up my mother then you call me to fix things. What did you do to upset her this time!"

Mom screamed can-can music, and Maurie screamed more noise. Maurie turned his head toward Mom and cried as he watched her dance her way in from the kitchen. "What did they do to you?" he sobbed. Mom didn't even look at Maurie.

Maurie turned his head to me. "I hate all of you! Look at all the problems you caused my mother!" Maurie turned to Dad, "You caused all these problems for my mother! You and those kids, and the neighbors and her doctors! She would be fine if it wasn't for all of you!"

Maurie never liked our neighbors. He never liked anyone who complained about his Mom. He always acted as if she was his mother only, and Johnny and I didn't belong here. He didn't like her doctors either because they told him that Mom would never be normal. Maurie told them that she was normal and it was only because of Dad, me, Johnny, and the neighbors that she always acted up.

Maurie stiffened up like a wind-up toy and clomped out of the house slamming the door. For a moment I thought the door window would break. Some help Maurie was. Dad never seemed to learn. And the more Dad called Maurie, the more Maurie hated all of us, especially Johnny. It was as if Maurie's hate was so big it couldn't all fit on one person.

Only a short while passed and there was laughter at the door. It was Mom's sisters and brother. I wished I could have called Dad's family, but I knew he would have been upset. Dad got up off the couch, opened the front door, and greeted them by saying, "She won't cook for me."

"Yeah, that was a great ball game," Mom's brother Abe said to Aunt Belle. "Oh hi," they said to Dad. They rushed past me not saying a word, and flopped their fat bodies down on the chairs as if eager to see the show.

I went into the corner of the room and sat on the floor. I was in the corner that bordered between the living room and dining room. I could see everything and everyone, but they all acted as if they couldn't see me. Johnny walked slowly down the stairs and into the living room. He looked at the audience, and went outside.

I felt like a little ant sitting in the corner. They all liked Mom's shows except for Uncle Abe's wife, Martha. She always complained about having to visit us. They were all middle-aged fat elephants with fat legs hanging over the chairs. Mom danced her way into the living room from the kitchen with a towel wrapped around her like a belly dancer.

"She's pretty good at dancing," said Aunt Rebecca, who had sunk comfortably into the soft foam-stuffed arm chair. She had the best seat in the house for watching the show. She sat there in her freshly ironed dress, and her long black hair neatly combed back into a bun. Her nails were always polished. She had a different look about her than Mom. Aunt Rebecca was a well groomed circus elephant.

Mom unwrapped the towel and peed on the rug. They all laughed. I wished they would have all dropped dead. The elephants loved watching the monkey. Aunt Martha was the only one not laughing. She looked angry and wrinkled up her nose at Uncle Abe.

He looked back at her. "Where's your sense of humor?" He pulled out a cigar from his shirt pocket and puffed away, trying to make smoke rings.

Dad sobbed, "I'm afraid she'll run outside and the neighbors will see her."

"Don't worry," said Aunt Belle, giving Dad a sad look, "We'll take care of her."

Dad walked out of the room crying. As soon as he was out of sight, Aunt Belle's sad look burst into witch's laughter. I wished I could have taken a douche bag and shoved it down her cackling throat.

"This is fun," she said to Aunt Rebecca.

I hated adults. I never wanted to be one of them. I looked at Mom as she danced around nude. How ugly her body was. Her fat boobs stuck out like stubs of deformed arms that never finished growing. If I ever grew boobs, I would cut them off! I never wanted to look like her. I hated her. The girls at school couldn't wait till they grew boobs. I didn't know why they wanted to be ugly. I never wanted to grow up and be like Mom and her family. Never would I grow up.

"Don't let the neighbors see her," Dad cried out from the kitchen to everyone.

"Don't worry," Aunt Belle yelled to him. "Just lock the doors."

I crawled a few steps along the floor toward the kitchen to see what Dad was doing. I figured he must be eating something, and I wondered what. I was hungry too. I was a small ant that no one noticed. I peeped into the kitchen. Dad swept up the broken dishes that Mom had can-canned with. I didn't want to stay and help him, so I crawled back to my corner, and listened to Belle and Rebecca.

"It's so nice when we're all together like this," said Aunt Rebecca. "It's just like when we were kids."

Oh, so even they would rather be kids.

Aunt Belle laughed, "I'll go make some coffee."

"Two sugars with mine," Uncle Abe yelled out.

Adults drink that black stuff.

"Hey! Any coffee cake in the house?" Uncle Abe yelled to Aunt Belle.

"No. I can't find anything," said Aunt Belle.

Dad came into the living room where Mom still danced. He sat on the couch and looked at the floor. Aunt Martha went into the kitchen. She looked around, opened up all the cupboards and slammed them one by one. She opened the refrigerator, stuck her head in, looked around, and slammed that too.

"Martha! You go out and get some coffee cake," commanded Uncle Abe as he tossed her the car keys.

"Why should I have to buy the food!" she snapped. "I think I'll just go home and leave you here with the rest of your family."

"Come on, Martha. Just get some cake and sugar."

Aunt Martha huffed in anger, "Sugar and cake." She squeezed the car keys in her fist, as if she were trying to strangle them.

"Can you get some food for us too?" I asked her.

"How am I supposed to know what kind of food kids eat! Go ask your father for food." Out the door she went with Uncle Abe's keys.

Dad looked at Mom, then turned to Aunt Belle. "Maybe you can make her get dressed."

"Oh, it's O.K. She's the baby in the family. Let her do as she wants," answered Aunt Belle.

"In the morning I have to go to work. Don't let her out."
Dad sniffed and blew his nose in his hanky.

"Don't worry. You go to work, and we'll stay here till she
snaps out of it or you or Maurie decide to take her to a
hospital."

Aunt Rebecca laughed. "It's good for people when they let
loose, dance, and pee off their anxieties"

Johnny and I went down to the basement and ate hot dogs
and potato chips that Aunt Martha brought back for us. The
basement was damp but it was our own private hideaway.
We were a couple of refugees. We stayed down there and
slept on the floor while the grown-ups partied. We knew that
eventually, Dad or Maurie would take Mom to the hospital.
That's what always happened.

Chapter 8 - Splat

Johnny and I were walking home from school. We were on a main street but at 3:30 there was hardly any traffic. It was a sunny day and looked warm, but the day was lying. It was cold, about 40 degrees. I watched the leaves on the trees shiver in the breeze.

Suddenly we were surrounded by a mob of about 15 kids spitting at us. Splat! Like rats they poured out of their hiding places. "Nigger !" they yelled, "There's Nigger and his white sister!" Splat! Splat ! I grabbed Johnny's hand. "Run!"

They were chasing us. Their cheeks puffed up to make spit. They looked like gnawing rats. It rained spit and stones. "Nigger! Nigger!"

"Quick, Johnny!" I yelled. "The short cut through the alley." We made a fast turn down the skinny alley, and ran through the maze of garbage cans. I heard a scream from Johnny. I turned my head. A rock gouged his face. Blood came from his nose and cheek. I heard the rats laughing as they tossed over garbage cans that blocked their way. So many rats laughing. There was no time to stop and fix Johnny's face. We kept running. The rats were now happy with just tossing over garbage cans and laughing. I took one of Johnny's hands and pulled him. His other hand covered his face and all that blood. We ran down the alley till we reached our house. I let go of his hand to reach into my pocket for the house key. I pushed the door open and Johnny ran in and over to the kitchen sink. He slipped his face under the faucet of cold water.

"What's all the noise?" Mom said as she walked in. Mom had spent the day lying around on the couch. I could tell from the way her dress looked like a crunched up dust rag, and none of her hairs seem to go in the same direction.

"The kids at school called Johnny Nigger again, and one of them threw a rock."

Mom walked to the refrigerator. I wondered if she was going to fix herself a cold drink while Johnny bled. She opened the freezer section and took out some ice cubes. "Here," she said. "Use ice." I grabbed a cube and put it on Johnny's cheek. He jumped away from me, and screamed.

"I didn't mean to hurt you, Johnny."

Mom stiffened her fist and stared at Johnny. She took a step towards Johnny as if she were about to beat him with her fist. "Who the hell told you to be born black anyway!" she bellowed out. "You're a freak, Johnny! I wish you would die!!" She turned around and stomped back into the living room.

Johnny leaned over the sink, running cold water down his face. I stood motionless. I heard Mom making a phone call, and wondered who she could be calling. She didn't have any friends. Johnny lifted his head out of the sink. "Jill, put the ice away. Cold water is good enough."

"OK. I didn't mean to hurt you."

"Is this Grace Hospital?" Mom said to whomever she was talking to. "I came to you to have a baby, and you gave me a freak! You gave me the wrong baby! You better check your records! You gave me a black baby!"

My throat stiffened. I felt so embarrassed when Mom did stuff like that. I hated it when people found out she was my mother. I wished I could have told people that it was a big mistake. She was really just a stranger that I met on the street. And Johnny, how he must have felt. He looked into the sink and poured cold water on his face. He didn't say anything, but I knew he heard her. He was so cute. I loved his big brown eyes and curly hair. He wasn't a freak. Mom was.

"Well, you check your records and call me back!" Mom

demanded from whomever she was talking to. I wished Johnny and I could run away somewhere, but there was no place to go. Finally, she hung up. I heard her go back to the couch and flop down. "He's a freak!" she howled. "They gave me a freak!" "Johnny!" she screamed, who told you to be a freak?! WHO!"

Johnny looked awful. His face stopped bleeding, but he had a purple bruise on his nose and was cut on the cheek, and his whole face was so sad.

I tugged Johnny's arm. "I know what Johnny, let's go outside and wait in the yard till Dad gets home. We'll leave Mom inside on the couch."

"Leave me alone," he cried. He pulled away from me and ran past Mom and up the stairs to the bedrooms. He slammed the bedroom door, and the whole house shook. I sneaked out the back door to the yard, but there was nothing I could do but wait. I wished I were a little animal that could dig holes in the ground and hide. The garage! I could be like a puppy hiding in its puppy house. I roamed in and sat on the floor with my paws on my knees and looked out the tiny window where sunlight kisses the top of my head. I moved around in the sunlight and let it stroke my head. But what next? No one could expect this pup to sit here all day. I hoped Johnny was O.K. Hoped he wasn't up there crying.

I quietly crawled out of my shelter, and sneaked back into the house. Softly and silently I passed through the living room where Mom slept on the couch. The couch stretched out, like a yawning cat, along the wall where the windows faced the front yard. Slowly, I crept up each of the brown carpeted stairs toward the bedrooms. *Careful, I told me. One step at a time. OK, now where's Johnny. He wasn't in his room.* I walked into my room. There he was, in my room standing in front of my full length mirror that was attached to the front of my closet door, and he was wearing the dress that I was supposed to wear to school the next day.

"Johnny!" my voice screamed out in a whisper. I didn't dare talk in a normal voice and risk waking Mom. "Not again, Johnny! How can you do this to me?" In my clothes Johnny seemed to feel safe. "Johnny! I have enough problems without other kids laughing at me because my clothes are torn and dirty. You always tear my dresses trying to get them on." Johnny stood there looking at himself in the mirror and didn't even look at me. "Johnny! Can't you hear me?!" No, of course not. He wasn't Johnny when he dressed that way. "Get out of my clothes! Dad will be here soon. Don't you care?!"

I heard Dad's car pull up in the driveway. Johnny stopped flirting with himself in the mirror and changed back to his own clothes. We both went back downstairs. We walked past Mom on the couch and went toward the kitchen. The kitchen was always the first place Dad went. He was pudgy with a baby face. "Hi Dad," I said. Dad picked up the lid of a pot on the stove. He was checking to see if any food was being cooked. He placed the lid back on the pot. There must have been something in there.

He looked at us. "How come your face is like that, Johnny?"

Johnny stood there. He didn't talk. He just looked at the floor as if it were his fault.

"The kids beat him up again and called him Nigger," I explained.

Mom wandered in and looked at Dad as if she were about to attack him. "'Who told him to be a freak! Who told him to be black!"

"He's not black," Dad answered. "It's the god damn principal's fault! I've been to those PTA meetings. She always talks how she hates black people and doesn't want any in the school. She lets kids think that Johnny is black. I'm going to tell her off! I'm going to school with you kids tomorrow and I'm going to tell that bitch off! It's her fault the kids think Johnny is black! He can't be black! He's our kid!"

I washed and ironed one of my dresses then neatly folded it into a large grocery bag. I hid the bag under the kitchen sink.

I woke up early the next morning and ran to the sink to retrieve my dress. The bag and dress were wrinkled and smelled of Johnny. There was no time to wash it again. I heard Mom, Dad, and Johnny getting up. I put on my dress and got ready. The whole family squashed into Dad's car and we drove to school. We walked in. The building seemed dark after being outside in cold but blinding sunlight. It always took time for my eyes to adjust to the indoor school lighting. There were no windows in the hallways, just the dim electric lights overhead that seemed to get brighter after a while.

We were about 15 minutes early, but as soon as the bell rings, Johnny and I would have to go to our classes. I smelled bad. I could tell. My dress smelled from Johnny's sweat. But this was the only dress I had to wear. All my clothes are dirty. It didn't matter where I put my clean clothes. Johnny found them like a cockroach finds food.

We all marched up to the principal's office. The door was open. She was a fat woman sitting behind her fat desk with a skinny lamp. She was busy writing something and didn't see us. She had so much starch in her blouse that it looked like cardboard. She wore enough hair spray in her brown-gray hair that it too looked starched.

"You bitch!" Dad yelled as he walked in and went to the edge of her desk.

She looked up and dropped her pen. Her whole body jerked as if she were hit by lightning. Mom followed Dad and stood right behind him. Johnny and I stood at the door and watched. The principal stared at Dad. She didn't say a word.

"Look at Johnny's face!" Dad yelled. But the principal didn't look. She kept staring at Dad.

"See what you did," he yelled.

She didn't even turn her head to look. Her eyes didn't leave Dad. "You damn bitch! The kids beat up Johnny and called him Nigger, He's my son! He's not black! You better do something! He's not black, I tell you! You god damn bitch! He's my kid." Dad kept yelling as he turned to the door.

"Come on," he said to Mom. "I have to get to the factory." He walked out of the door. Mom followed. They walked past Johnny and me and through the long hallway toward the door of the building. The principal got up and walked to her office door. Her eyes stared at Dad. As soon as she saw him and Mom leave the building, her stiffened starched body fell limp. Her predators were gone. They stomped out though the small door at the end of the long hallway that led into the blinding outside. The principal gently rubbed her finger along her eyebrow as she walked past Johnny and me on her way back to her desk. I smelled her perfumed hair spray as she passed by. She always smelled like a garden full of flowers. Close up, it was more like insecticide. She sat down, picked up her pen and continued to write whatever it was she was writing. The bell rang and Johnny and I left for class. I smelled bad. I smelled Johnny's sweat all over me.

Chapter 9 - Mom's Underwear

It was the season for planting seeds and plants along the green wooden post-fence that stood guard at the border of our back yard. Every week end Dad was out there.

I stood nearby watching him as he prepared little cribs for his tomato plants, then neatly tucked them in with soil. He smiled at them, "See my nice plants." He admired them instead of me. I felt like a step child.

I sat down on the grass and let the sun hug me with its warmth. Dad smiled at his radishes. The sound of a lawnmower on the other side of the fence pulled my mind away from Dad. Mr. McKinley was mowing with his hand mower I watched through the fence posts as he pushed it back and forth over his grass that he had worked so hard to grow. His mower was a noisy grass eater, and I couldn't help but watch him as he pushed and pulled. He was a thin man with short brown hair, and when he wasn't working at his job, he was working on his house. He always liked things looking clean and neat.

"My radishes look pretty good," I heard Dad say, I think to the tomato plants. Right then Mom came out through the back door. She walked up to Dad and handed him a glass of lemonade. She was barefoot. In fact, she was mostly bare. She only had on a bra and underpants. Her boobs looked like they were trying to crawl out of her bra. Dad smiled at the glass of lemonade then gulped it down.

'When will you be done?" she asked Dad, "We need to get groceries."

"Just give me a couple minutes," he answered as he handed Mom the glass.

Mr. McKinley looked at Mom then quickly looked the other way, set his mower down and hurriedly walked toward his house. Mom walked over to the fence, leaned her elbow on it and yelled out, "Hi, Mr. McKinley. What are you doing?" He kept his head down and kept walking toward his back door. He always went into his house whenever Mom came outside, even when he was in the middle of working. Mom stood at the fence. Her eyes and her boobs stared out in puzzlement at Mr. McKinley.

"Maybe he doesn't like seeing you in your underwear, Mom."

"Nonsense!" she snapped, "He's a married man. He's used to seeing a woman in underwear. Besides, I can do what I want. This is my yard."

I didn't say another word. I just looked at Dad as he brushed off some soil from his trowel. "There," he said, "We can go shopping now."

"Good," Mom said, "I'll go get my shoes and a dress."

I watched her as she went though the back door and into the house. Then I glanced over the fence to Mr. McKinley's house. I saw him at his kitchen window looking out at us. Dad was brushing off soil from the knees of his slacks.

"Dad, aren't you embarrassed about the way Mom doesn't dress?"

"Yeah," he said, as he straightened out his slacks. "But we can't tell Mom what to do." He looked at his plants, "My radishes are really good."

I wasn't sure what to think. I noticed that many of the neighbor ladies came outside barefoot, dressed only in shorts and pullover tank tops. They're not covered much more than Mom is. Yet, I notice their faces when Mom walks around in underwear.

"If you can't do anything about Mom, I wish you would at least do something to help Johnny. He has no friends."

"The tomato plants are looking real good too," he answered.

"Johnny is up in his room, just sitting and doing nothing. I wish you'd help him."

"I think I'll plant some more green onions." He smiled at his plants like a proud father, then went into the house. A few minutes later he and Mom came out, and got into the car. He waved to me as they drove off.

Chapter 10 - Tramp

"Mom," I called out as I entered the house from school. "Do we have any cake mix in the house? I need to bring some cup cakes to school tomorrow for our glee club party. We're singing at the school assembly and each member needs to bring something for a party afterward."

Mom searched through the cupboards, but couldn't find a mix. "Jill, get out the sugar and cocoa. We'll make it from scratch. There won't be time in the morning, so let's do it now. We can keep them in the freezer till morning."

We made great cup cakes. Then she started on dinner. As soon as the cup cakes came out of the oven, I grabbed a few and took them outside for Johnny and me.

"Tramp!" I heard Mom yell to someone as I reentered the house through the back door. I walked into the living room where she was staring out the window.

"Tramp!" she yelled again. I wondered if she was talking to the window. I didn't see anyone outside except the neighbor across the street who was pulling out weeds from her front lawn. Mom stood by the window with her hands on her hips. "Jill, just look at that tramp!"

I think she was referring to the neighbor's weeds. Mom glanced over to me, "You see that, Jill. Look at that tramp across the street."

"What tramp? All I see is Mrs. Ferson pulling weeds."

"Look at her! Look at those tight pants she's wearing! I'd never go out like that!"

"What do you mean? You go out in your underwear."

"You shut up! I would never do that!"

I decided to go back outside and play with Johnny. We went down the street to an empty lot where there was an old apple tree. Johnny climbed up and tossed some apples down. We came back just as Dad was pulling up in his car. We all went into the house together. The house smelled of pot roast and garlic. Mom stood at the stove cooking, using all four burners. Vegetables in one pot, roast in another, squash in a third, and chocolate pudding in the fourth. Dad stood next to Mom and looked in all the pots.

"Everything is ready to eat," he declared. He grabbed some dishes and silverware and put them on the table. Johnny and I sat down.

"Not so fast!" Mom yelled at all of us. "You're my ward! I'm the head nurse around here!"

"0.K.," Dad said. "Let's eat."

He took the pot with the roast and brought it to the table. Johnny and I helped ourselves. Dad returned with the vegetables and squash, and Mom set the pudding on the table.

"I didn't say you could eat yet," Mom yelled. "I'm the ward nurse here."

"O.K.," Dad said meekly, "Let's just eat."

Johnny and I finished our meat, and started on the pudding. We always ate vegetables last.

"It's too hot in here," Mom said. She slipped her dress off, folded it over a chair, and went to open windows all over the house.

"Dad," I whispered, "Mom doesn't know who she is."

He burst into laughter, "Of course she knows who she is. Everyone knows who she is."

"But Dad, she thinks we're her ward. She doesn't know who we are."

"Of course she knows who we are. We all know who we are."

I looked at Johnny. All he seemed to care about was the pudding he was shoveling down.

"But Dad," I continued, "She said she's a nurse."

Dad laughed. "Lots of people say things, Jill."

Mom came back into the room. She was barefoot and only wore her half slip which she had pulled up over her boobs and the hem barely covered her thighs. She sat down and ate.

After dinner, Mom went outside on the porch wearing only her half slip. I heard her yell at somebody but I'm not sure who. She shouted at someone for being a tramp, and yelled out something about being in charge, because she was the head nurse.

Chapter 11 - Ducks

"Two baby ducks hatched from eggs, and Sara, a girl at school has been keeping them as pets. But now her family is going on summer vacation, so she has to get rid of them. It's O.K., Dad, if I take them from her, isn't it?" I said. "It's just for the summer."

Dad had just walked in from work and was looking in the pots on the stove to see if any food was being cooked. "Looks like spaghetti," he said.

"What about the ducks? I can bring them home tomorrow. And we can let them live in the back yard. Wouldn't you like some pet ducks?"

"What if Mom doesn't like the ducks? What's she going to say if she sees ducks in the yard?"

"It will be O.K. Mom's been busy lately lying around on the couch. She doesn't come out to the yard that much anyway. Besides the ducks don't have anywhere else to go and we have a big yard."

"How are we going to explain ducks to Mom?"

Mom walked into the kitchen from the living room. She wore her wrinkled-up house dress with the pink and red flowers on it. Her hair was decorated with bobby pins. "What's this you said about ducks?"

"I'm going to bring home a couple baby ducks tomorrow. And Dad said it would be O.K."

Dad looked at Mom like a scared little kid and didn't say anything

"It's O.K." I rattled on. "They're just babies. They won't take up much space and Johnny said we could use his old plastic bucket to make a swimming pool for them. It's O.K. Right Mom?"

She shrugged her right shoulder, picked up the lid of one

of the pots on the stove, and sniffed the food. "I don't care what you do."

"Great!" I ran out to explain to Johnny that we're going to use his old plastic bucket for a duck pool.

The next day, I walked with Sara to her house after school.

"Are those ducks 2 girls, 2 boys, or one of each?" I asked.

"I don't know. We got them from a farmer that my dad knows, but he didn't tell us what they were."

"It will be fun having your ducks."

"I was going to give them to Barbara, but her parents said, NO! And we only have two more days till school is out and we go on vacation. So I'm glad your parents like ducks."

We got to Sara's house. Her mom was quite pretty and I wished my mom looked like her. She wore a cream silky blouse with a gold necklace and earrings, a brown skirt and brown shoes. Her hair looked as if she had just returned from the beauty shop.

Sara's family had a special fenced off area in their yard where they were keeping the ducks. There was even a little wading pool with a fountain. Those ducks had been living like millionaires. Her mom scooped up the ducks, one at a time, and put them in a big brown box. Then we put the box in the back seat of her station wagon, and the three of us got in the front. As we drove home, I heard quacking in the back seat.

We pulled into the driveway, and Sara's mom helped me carry the duck box into the yard.

"Enjoy your pets," she said. "Be sure to lock the gate before you let them out of the box." She went back to the car where Sara was still waiting. I waved goodbye as they backed out of the driveway.

I locked the yard gate and gently tipped the box. Two ducks jumped out. I ran into the house for crayons and paper.

Mom was lying on the couch but she wasn't asleep. I tried to be quiet as I passed her and was hoping she wouldn't want to go to the yard. Just then Johnny came running out of his room.

"Are the ducks here?"

"Yep." I said. "But, be careful to keep the gate locked."

"O.K." And he ran outside.

I finished writing with my crayons and went outside to tape my sign on the gate. BEWARE OF DUCKS

Johnny and I sat on the grass and watched our ducks run around the yard.

"They're eating Dad's tomato plants!" Johnny said. "I'll run inside and get some bread for them."

He raced into the house and came back out with a whole loaf. He ripped open the wrapper, pulled out a slice, and started tearing it in pieces. The ducks ran up to him and grabbed it out of his hand. He jumped back and dropped the whole loaf.

"I hope Mom wasn't planning to use that bread for dinner," I told him. We continued sitting on the grass watching our ducks eat and play. They jumped in and out of the bucket full of water that Johnny set up for them. Then one chased the other around on the grass. Johnny got up and chased both of them. He became a duck. He stopped to rest and stared at the other ducks.

"I think Dad is going to be mad when he sees what the ducks just did on the grass," he said.

"It's O.K. Dad was going to buy fertilizer anyway."

"He'll be home any minute. I think I'll go to my room and play."

Dad drove up in front of the house, got out of the car, slammed the door like he always does, and walked through the gate and into the yard. I sat on the grass with the ducks.

"Are those the ducks!" he asked as he stared at them.

"Yep."

"You told me they were baby ducks."

"They are babies. They're only a few months old."

"But you said they were babies that hatched from eggs."

"They did hatch from eggs."

"But I thought they were babies."

"They are. They're only three months old. I told you, Sara has been keeping them as pets, right up till now, when she's going on vacation."

I looked at my puffy white ducks as they ran around Dad's vegetable garden. "I guess ducks do grow kind of fast."

Dad looked at the ducks, the grass, and his garden. I looked at Dad's face. I knew he wanted to cry.

Chapter 12 - The Heater

Seasons come and seasons go and I had become a teenager. My 13th and 14th birthdays were like funerals. I cried. I was now too old to be adopted and loved. I wanted to be a baby forever. Yet, I also wished I could go off to exciting places and do exciting things.

I peddled around all day on my bike and pretended that it could take me far away to other countries. Thoughts of Johnny and me riding on camels in the Arabian Desert filled my mind. We would build sandmen and have sandball fights. Our camels would think we were Arabs because we would be dressed in Arab clothes, with kitchen towels hanging over our heads. Someday I'll go far away, I told myself.

In my dreams, I was always running off somewhere. Sometimes to the ocean where I swam with the seals, or to the jungle where I ate bananas with the monkeys. But, some of my dreams shook me out of my sleep. I saw babies with their arms and legs cut off and thrown into baskets. I saw people on fire. Their skins peel off. Their bodies crumble into ashes. I run away. Someone chases me. I run fast but it's never fast enough. I'm grabbed, stabbed, and chopped to pieces.

The cold autumn breeze rubbing against my face made me want to stop peddling and go inside. It was only because of Johnny that I had lingered so long. He was making a surprise for me with some craft supplies that he brought home from school, and he didn't want me around.

I crept into the house and passed the bathroom where Mom was messing with the wall heater. She had the protective cover unscrewed. So, she found something to play with, I thought. It works fine, but she'll probably end up breaking it.

I went to Johnny's room, "Aren't you done with my surprise yet?" I asked.

"Nope!" He smiled. His face made dimples, and his mouth showed off all his teeth.

"Come on, Sis," he said. "Take your shoes off and stand on this paper. I need to trace your feet."

I kept bugging him to tell me what he was making, but he was determined not to tell.

"You'll see when I finish," he said.

I stood on the paper while he traced my feet with a big green crayon. He giggled and I felt a bit foolish because I was sure he was going to play some kind of joke on me.

"You're sure putting a lot of time into making that thing," I said.

At first, I thought he was making me a dog collar because I saw him cut some leather into thin strips. But then I caught him tracing a pair of my shoes. And now it was my feet.

His smile blossomed across his face. "It's a surprise," he said. "Now go and let me finish."

Obviously, he was making something special, but I couldn't figure out what.

I looked out his bedroom window at the sky. Clouds floated around but they hadn't landed yet. I really didn't want to go back outside, but I was anxious for him to finish my surprise. I left the room, quietly passed the bathroom where Mom still entertained herself, and went outside.

There by a mud puddle stood my bike and I jumped on it like a cowboy, "O.K., horsy, you had enough time to drink. Now giddyup! Let's go!" We rode around in a circle, "Come on. Out of the corral," I said. "Let's go out front. Giddiyup!"

My bike was a good playmate, though I longed for a human friend. The girls in my class thought I was strange and I thought of them as a bunch of dumb pea brains. I rode around, thinking about their eagerness to wear lipstick and bras which made them look like clowns. We were all fourteen, but they tried to look their mother's age. They didn't understand that being grown up meant they no longer had a home. My mom couldn't wait for me to grow up so I could be forced into the streets.

The kids at school laughed at me. They said I dressed in baby clothes. They laughed at my shoes. "Baby shoes," they said, because they were tie shoes instead of slip-ons. They wore puffy hair, making their heads look swollen. They looked so dumb. I wore my hair in a pony tail with ribbons.

I wondered if Johnny was finished with my surprise. I talked to my bike and patted its handle bar. "Come on," I said, "back to the water hole." When I moseyed into the house, Mom was still busying herself like a baby with a new toy. I went up to Johnny's door. "Hi!" I shouted,

He jumped up from his desk and with both hands he hid something behind his back, That big grin was on his face again. "It's finished, Jill! Your surprise is finished!"

"Why are you still hiding it?"

He chuckled. "Which hand do you think it's in?"

"Oh boy, the left one."

He brought both hands out in front of him and in each hand was a moccasin. Beautiful leather moccasins covered with fringe! Two little blue pearl beads on each toe. I untied my shoes, pulled them off, and slipped on my new moccasins. "Johnny, they're beautiful! How did you get them to fit so perfectly?"

"I'm just good." He giggled as he looked down at my feet.

"What made you decide on moccasins?"

"I don't like those girls making fun of your tie shoes."

Mom's voice roared out of the bathroom. "Johnny! Come here, I need you to fix something."

I followed Johnny to the bathroom where Mom stood next to the heater. Stiff wires stuck out like hair full of hair spray, Mom glared at Johnny. "I want you to fix this. I just turned the power back on, so you can fix the heater for me, Johnny."

He stood there looking at the tile floor.

"Fix it for me, Johnny. You do want me to be proud of you, don't you?"

"O.K.," he said, as he stepped toward the heater.

"No!" I screamed. I grabbed him and pulled. "It's dangerous! Let's go outside!"

"Nonsense!" Mom snapped.

She smiled as she turned to Johnny. "It's just a heater. Now be a good son and fix it."

He pulled away from me. I grabbed his arm, and pulled. My heart punched at my insides.

Mom looked at him. "Be a good boy. You do want me to love you, don't you?"

He looked at her, then me, then the floor and didn't say anything, She grabbed his other arm, and yanked him toward the heater. "Be a good son to your mother!" She said as she pulled him to the wires.

I pulled his right arm. She pulled his left. I saw Johnny's face. He was crying, We were breaking his arms! I was stuck. If I ran for help to a neighbor it would be too late. I couldn't leave Johnny. Not for one second!

"You're too close! Don't touch!" I screamed.

Dad. I heard Dad. He finally got home!

"What's the screaming? I'm hungry," he said.

I kept screaming, He walked into the bathroom. Mom let go of Johnny, and he came crashing into me. Both of us fell on the floor. Mom stood there looking at Dad calmly, as if she didn't know why I had been screaming.

"Why the screaming?" Dad asked. Johnny and I picked ourselves up. Before I could answer, Dad saw the heater.

"Who the hell's been playing with the heater?! Those are live wires sticking out! Someone could get killed! Johnny you did this!"

Dad grabbed Johnny by his shirt collar and was about to slug him.

"Mom did it!" I yelled. "It wasn't Johnny!"

Mom stood there with her smile and didn't say anything. Dad looked at her, and his angry face went blank. He looked around the room as if he were lost. He looked up at the light bulb, above the green sink, then across the room along the ceiling and down to the green sunken tub. He stared into it as if he didn't know what it was. He lifted his head and looked around to where the walls met the ceiling. It was as if he had never seen the bathroom before. He turned to the heater.

"By golly," he exclaimed. "Something's wrong with the heater. I'll call a repair man after dinner. Let's eat, I'm hungry."

I stared at Dad but didn't say anything. He walked out the door and we all followed him to the kitchen. The smell of meatloaf and garlic poured out of the oven as Mom took it out and served us. I sat between Dad and Johnny. Mom sat on the other side of the table. I bit into something hard. A chip of burger bone, I thought. I spit it out. It was a sewing needle. I grasped it between my fingers and held it up to Dad. "Dad! Look! "

"Sh,,,," he said. "Don't start up with Mom."

He continued to stuff his mouth. I looked across the table at Mom. She was eating her food. I looked at Johnny. He was looking at his food and picking at it. He didn't seem to notice me looking at him. He was silent, not saying a word. I turned my head to Dad and watched him eat. There was something about the way he picked up his food with his hands and stuffed it into his mouth that reminded me of a baby in a high chair.

Chapter 13 - The Relatives Again

I had walked home from school in the rain in wet mushy shoes. I might as well have taken them off and gone barefoot. I don't know. Does it make sense to go barefoot, I wondered. Should I protect my shoes or are they supposed to protect me?

When I entered the house, the first thing I saw was Mom, sitting on the living room floor with her legs folded, singing nursery rhymes. She was wearing her bright red house-slippers. The hemline on her dress sat above her knees, so that her bare hairy legs were showing. She had a piece of green ribbon bobby-pinned in her hair. Her eyes stared at her hands as they danced in front of her in rhythm with her singing. I walked past her, trying not to get too close. Her staring eyes found me, and she dropped her hands to her folded knees and stopped singing.

"You keep the snow out of my shoe!" she demanded.

"It's 60 degrees out," I told her. She jumped up and stared at me. Her dancing hands became fists. I should have known better than to say anything. My heart pounded against my chest as if it wanted to get out of my body and run away. I turned to the door and ran outside and into the garage, hoping Dad would get home soon.

The garage was my refuge, its tiny window my peephole. Sometimes Dad was afraid to come home. I hoped this wouldn't be one of those times. From the peephole, I could watch the driveway and the house. Johnny came running up to the door of the house crying.

"Johnny!" I called out. "Don't go in the house. Come here to the garage."

He had his right hand over his stomach and was breathing hard. "The kids kicked me in the stomach and called me "Nigger," I want to go lie down."

"Just lie down here in the garage. I'll go out front and watch for Dad."

I paced back and forth on the curve in front of the house. Finally Dad's car came, pulled up in front of me, and he got out. "I'm hungry, Jill. Let's go in and eat."

"Mom is acting up," I told him.

"Oh, just ignore her. Let's go eat."

Dad went into the house and I followed him slowly, very slowly. Mom stood on the kitchen table wearing only a half slip.

"I'm the queen!" she yelled. "You bow down to me!"

"Why do you have to act like that?" Dad pouted.

"Dad, maybe you should take her to the hospital again?"

"There's nothing wrong with Mom," he snapped. "She just likes to act up! What's for supper?" He looked on the stove but there wasn't anything there. "I'm hungry," he complained.

"Dad, we need to help Johnny. He's in the garage lying down. The kids kicked him and called him, "Nigger" again."

"Johnny isn't a nigger. He'll outgrow it. Leave me alone, Jill. Can't you see how Mom is acting to me? She doesn't even care if I eat."

Mom took off her half slip and threw it at Dad. It was as if she were sleepwalking but there was no way to ever wake her. The slip hit Dad's forehead and fell to the floor. His face stiffened and he put his hand over his eyes. I saw tears leaking out.

I wished Dad would have never married Mom. I wished his mother wouldn't have died. I wished that Dad could have had some friends to call. I didn't have any friends who I could call.

Johnny walked into the house, but didn't look at any of us. He went straight upstairs, passing Mom as if he didn't notice she was naked and yelling. He looked tired.

I went to the stairway, half way to Johnny's room and half

way from where Dad stood. I felt stuck, I didn't know what to say to Dad, I stood there for several minutes, then walked towards Johnny's room. "Johnny? Are you O.K.?" I asked as I entered his bedroom, but he wasn't there. "Johnny, where are you?"

I walked over to my room. "Johnny!" I screamed. He was wearing my Navy sailor blouse with gold trim and gold buttons, and my blue wool skirt. My blouse was ripped at the sleeves, and one button was lying on the floor. I felt it was me that was ripped.

"Johnny! Can't you hear me?!"

He kept looking at himself in the mirror as if I weren't there. My brown cotton dress lay lifeless and wrinkled on the floor. I walked over to it. It was stained and smelled from Johnny's sweat. I picked it up and held it in my arms as if it were a dead baby. "You creep, Johnny! I have nothing to wear to school!"

Johnny gazed into the mirror and acted as if he didn't hear me. I laid my dress across my bed. Johnny's eyes watched the mirror. I could see that dressing in my clothes was some kind of sickness. My eyes blurred with tears.

"Johnny, what if Mom finds out what you do?" I felt the tears drip down my cheeks. I hugged Johnny. "How can I keep protecting you?" Johnny didn't move.

I went out to the hallway. Dad came clomping up the stairs carrying a large paper shopping bag. He looked like a plump overgrown first grader with his lunch sack. I followed and watched as he pulled his clothes from his bedroom closet and stuffed them into his paper bag.

"Dad. What are you doing?"

"She doesn't love me," he sobbed. "So I'm leaving. I'll show her."

"Dad! Don't leave us!"

My heart beat fast, and my lungs gasped for more air. How could I manage with just Johnny and me? Just having Dad around to distract Mom helped. He had always told me that the day would come when he'd leave and not come back.

There was a loud smash downstairs. Mom must have butchered a window.

"Dad. Call a doctor."

"No, Jill. They'll just take her away again. It never helps."

"Call anyway. Don't leave us."

"I'll call her sisters and brother and Maurie," he said.

He went to the phone and dialed. I went back to my room where Johnny was still dressed in my sailor blouse, and blue wool skirt.

"You look like a clown!" I told him. I pulled my clothes off him, and he went back to his own room and own clothes, never saying a word. I jumped on my bed bouncing up and down, hugging my pillow and waiting.

I heard Maurie storm into the house. I put on my new moccasins. I went downstairs. There was Maurie all dressed up in a suit, with a blue tie and red face, and yelling at Dad.

Maurie turned his head to me. "I hate all of you! Look at all the problems you caused my mother! And look at you, Jill. You stink! Your clothes are always torn! I would die of embarrassment if anyone found out you were my sister!"

I looked down at the floor and wiggled my toes in my new moccasins. "I have new moccasins," I told Maurie. "Johnny made them."

"Oh, so that little shit can actually do something."

I explained to Maurie about Mom trying to kill Johnny with the electric heater. I hoped he would do something to help us. Instead he stood there looking at me, as if I had said something like, "It's a nice day."

"Well," he said. "We have to get rid of Johnny somehow. I

don't want a black brother. Everyone knows that Mom got pregnant with him in a mental hospital."

It never mattered to me. Johnny was still my brother.

"Hang on to those moccasins as a souvenir," Maurie continued. "You won't have Johnny much longer. It's more than time to get rid of him."

I looked at Maurie's face. It was calm, so matter of fact, as if he were talking about weather. He too belonged to the group of sleepwalkers.

"You won't have Johnny much longer. It's more than time to get rid of him."

Dad sat on the couch with his watery eyes looking down at the carpet. He mumbled something about his mother dying. I don't think he heard anything that Maurie was saying.

I looked down at my moccasins and curled my toes. I felt my face turning stiff.

"I don't know what you did to my mother, Jill, but I know you did something!"

Maurie looked at Dad. "You caused all these problems for my mother! You and those kids, and the neighbors and her doctors!"

"I never had nothing," Dad said. "The Nazis took my home."

Maurie ran out of the house and slammed the door. Only minutes later, Mom's family was at the door and Dad let the zoo in. Uncle Abe said something about his ball team. It must have been something funny because Aunt Belle laughed. They took their seats to watch the show. I went into the kitchen and stepped over the broken glass from the window that Mom had shattered. I grabbed bread and peanut butter and took it downstairs to the basement. That would be Johnny's and my home till Mom got sent to the hospital.

Chapter 14 - The Chemistry Lab

Mom's family partied all night. When Johnny and I left for school the next morning they were all asleep on the living room floor like a bunch of drunks. Mom's can-can music was still coming from her bedroom.

In the afternoon when my last class finished, I wandered into the high school chem lab just because it was empty, and I wanted to be alone. I was not eager to go home.

I closed the door behind me, shut off the lights, and climbed up on one of the metal work tables and sat in its center, with my legs folded. The surface felt cold, but I liked being on something high. There was a small gas burner on each table. I would have loved to have popcorn to pop. Those burners were great for that. All around me were shelves full of bottles, full of chemicals. Along one side of the lab were opened windows, and I could see the fresh-cut lawn outside and smell green through the air. I was a panther sitting on top of a mountain, looking out to the plains below.

The lab door opened and Pat, my classmate from gym, walked in. She carried a pile of books in her right arm, and was using her left arm to close the door behind her. Suddenly, her eyes swung from the door knob to me. She stared at me for a moment, looking at me as if I were a genie that had popped out of one of the bottles. I stared back.

"What are you doing here?" she asked.

"Just sitting. What are you doing?"

"I want to play a prank on the chem teacher. I was thinking of putting a goldfish into the distilled water tank, but I couldn't find any fish. I looked in the biology labs, but no fish. I don't suppose you have any ideas."

I looked around the room. There were all kinds of bottles of stuff that I didn't know what they were.

"Maybe we can just mix a little of everything in the lab

together to see if anything happens," I told her. "Maybe we'll find something that can turn the water into funny colors. Wouldn't it be fun to make the water blue? Or better yet, yellow, so it will look like someone peed in it."

She laughed, and grabbed a test tube. "O.K." she said, "Let's fill up the tube with some of everything."

"No." I said "Let's use the sink. If something explodes, we can turn the water on it."

"OK," she said.

We filled the sink with about an inch of water and started splashing drops of everything into it. She grabbed bottles. I grabbed bottles.

"So far the water just looks dirty and smells weird," I said. "But, there's lots of bottles so let's keep trying." We continued splashing. What's going to happen to you after you graduate?" I asked.

"I was going to go to the college here and live at home, but my parents decided to get a divorce, so I'm going away to Ferris State."

"Yeah, marriage can be a pretty bad thing," I told her.

"Well, my parents tried to make things work out. They went to counselors at the Jewish Family Service to get help."

"The Jewish Family Service?"

"Yeah, it's cheap. And they even see people for free sometimes. That's why my parents went there. My parents are always fighting over money. My dad is a real cheap skate."

I looked at the water. "The water looks dirty but still no color change."

"Let's start over with fresh water," she said.

"OK." And we pulled the plug. The drain gargled. And the icky stuff crawled down. We filled the sink with more water and grabbed more bottles. This time I grabbed some solid pellets. One bottle said *purified calcium* , and the other said *purified sodium.*

"Maybe I should just go out and buy some dye," she said. This stuff isn't working."

"But, we haven't finished trying." Some of the stuff did make the water smell bad.

I tossed in a few pellets. They fizzled up like a thousand bottles of soda pop opened all at once on a hot day. The smell was hurting my nose. I turned both bottles upside down and let all the pellets plop into the sink. We ran out slamming the door. I stopped to look through the door window. A big volcano erupted in the sink and sizzle was all over the lab. We ran.

Chapter 15 - Agencies

I thought about Pat and the Jewish Family Service, especially since she said sometimes they help people for free. I never did believe in religion, but my family was Jewish, so I decided to try them, too.

The big building was chopped up into tiny offices. On the main door was a white sign with blue letters J.F.S., for Jewish Family Service. I went up to the receptionist and asked to talk to someone. She looked through her big red book and said someone could see me in an hour and to come back then. I stayed and paced up and down the brown tiled hallway that led to closed brown doors. The receptionist told me I could read a magazine, but I continued to pace. Finally my turn came and I talked to a social worker in one of those tiny offices whose door I had paced by.

"What brings you to see me today?" Mrs. Kurtz asked. She was about 45 years old and a pleasant lady.

"My mother is a mental patient and causes a lot of trouble." I told her about Mom, then Johnny, then Maurie and Dad. She told me to come back the following Friday and meanwhile she would meet with other social workers. When I came back on Friday, she had me talk to two other social workers and they told me that they would call my parents. I was worried what would happen when they called, but it was a chance I had to take.

The following Monday evening they called the house. Dad answered. I stood nearby and listened. They invited Dad to come in with Mom. Dad never even asked why he was being invited. Mom didn't ask any questions either. She seemed to be in a deep daydream. I told Johnny what happened and he didn't say anything. I don't think he cared one way or the other.

A couple evenings later, our whole family went in

together, into that big building with small offices not much bigger than closets. We saw Mr. Weiner, a thin middle-aged man with thick glasses. His office didn't have any windows, but he had colorful pictures pasted on the walls. The one over his head was of a bright blue waterfall. We all sat around in brown chairs. Johnny and I pulled ours together. Mom wore a house dress and her hair was wrapped in bobby pins. She took the seat farthest away from everybody and hardly spoke. Dad was dressed up. He even wore a tie. He sat in the seat closest to Mr. Weiner, and Dad did all the talking. He started right in by announcing: "I've always worked hard, and I've always been a good kid. And I never took anything from anyone."

Dad sounded like a little boy pleading with his father to make things better.

Mr. Weiner looked at Dad, and asked him if he had any idea why he was invited in. Dad looked very confused, then laughed, "No, I don't know why I'm here." He sat in the chair, giggling like a little kid.

Mr. Weiner took several deep breaths. Dad kept giggling.

Mr. Weiner rubbed his forefinger and thumb along the edges of his eyeglasses.

"We're concerned about your kids," he said.

Dad giggled, "The kids are OK." Dad looked up at Mr. Weiner's face and continued on about how good he was as a kid. "I never stole anything," he said. "I never took anything from anybody."

Mr. Weiner took several more deep breaths as he rubbed his fingers along the edge of his eyeglasses, then up and down his cheeks.

Mom sat silently, resting on the chair as if she were home on the couch. Johnny looked bored. I looked up at the bright blue waterfall. Dad continued, "I work hard."

"Yes," said Mr. Weiner, "I know you're a hard worker. But right now we are worried about the kids."

Dad laughed, "The kids are O.K." he said. "It's just their mother who acts up."

"Yes, I know," sighed Mr. Weiner. "That's why I'm concerned about the kids."

Mr. Weiner sent us all out of the room except for Dad. I could hear Dad's giggling through the door. It must have been one of the funniest days in his life. Mom looked as if she were daydreaming. Her eyes crawled up and down the wall. Johnny walked over to the water fountain and leaned against it. I stood by the door and waited.

When the meeting ended, the door opened and Mr. Weiner and Dad came out. Dad was still giggling. Mr. Weiner pressed his lips together and tugged his hair.

There were several sessions like that. The only thing that changed was the social workers. Sometimes I went in by myself, and sometimes with the whole family. For Mom it was just another place to sit and rest. For Dad it was a chance to tell someone how good he was as a child, and complain about how Mom treated him.

The social workers kept telling me they would try to put Johnny and me into foster homes, but it wouldn't be easy as long as Dad said no. Dad said we didn't need foster homes just because Mom acts up. The social workers said that because Dad was able to hold down a job and support us, they couldn't legally take us away from him, but they kept trying to get him to sign consent forms. Dad did not understand why they wanted to move us out of the house. He laughed at the idea. He said it was crazy, and wondered why an agency wanted to meddle in his affairs. To him it was just people interfering with his life.

Then on a Sunday afternoon, Aunt Rebecca's married

daughter, Alena, called. I answered the phone. It was rare to hear from her. She lived in the suburbs and had two small kids. She told me that her husband was being transferred to California and they would be moving soon and that she would like to drop by and visit. She heard about all the parties Mom's family had been having at our house each time Mom went incoherent and started dancing. Aunt Rebecca had been in mental hospitals too. So Alena knew what it was like for us. I then called Mom to the phone so they could arrange Alena's visit. "Sure," I heard Mom say. "In a couple of hours. That will be fine." Mom hung up and went back to her bedroom.

When Alena came to the house, Dad was working in the yard. Mom was upstairs sleeping, and I was in the kitchen. I heard the door bell and walked to the living room. Johnny answered the door. "Hi, Alena," he said. He was wearing my blue shirtwaist dress with the buttons all the way down the front. He had bobby-pinned two green ribbons in his hair.

Alena stood there and stared at Johnny. She didn't say anything.

"Alena!" I shouted. "It's great to see you."

Dad came in from the yard and into the living room. "Have a seat," Dad told Alena. "Come on, sit down. You don't have to stand there. Make yourself at home."

Johnny went upstairs to his room. I don't think Dad noticed what he was wearing. Alena sat down on the couch, and I sat next to her.

"Where's your Mom?" she asked me.

"Sleeping. "

Dad looked at his dirty hands. "I better go wash up," he said. "I've been working in the yard all morning."

"Does Johnny always dress in your clothes?" Alena asked.

"Yep! I keep hiding clean clothes behind book shelves and behind desks, and sometimes under my bed, but in the morning when I need to get dressed for school, I find the clothes dirty. He sneaks into my room, when I'm not around and gets into everything. He's a giant cockroach. I asked Dad if he would put a lock on my door, but Dad said that would be a lot of work. And besides, he doesn't think I need a lock."

"I'm only going to be around for another couple months," Alena said. "I figure I can probably do something for you while I'm still here. But I don't want to get too involved either."

She looked a lot like Aunt Rebecca. Her dress was always ironed, her hair always combed, and her nails always polished. Yet, she was different than her mom. Alena didn't think Mom's parties were funny. And she didn't go into fits of depression.

Sometimes I thought that the more depressed Aunt Rebecca became the more she enjoyed Mom's parties, and the more she would encourage my mom to pee on the rug, or on the floor of the mental hospital. Many times Aunt Rebecca would accompany my mom to the hospital, and watch the party there too.

Dad came back into the room. "Good to see you, Alena. I'm always so busy around here. I spent all morning fixing up the yard. It should be time to eat now, but you see what kind of wife I have? She didn't fix anything! I've always been so good to her." Dad looked down at the floor. His face looked ready to cry.

"Looks like the whole family could use some help," Alena said. She lit a cigarette and puffed several puffs. "I know an agency where they can help Johnny. They do counseling."

I turned my head to avoid Alena's cigarette smoke.

Dad giggled. "We don't need agencies," he said, as he flopped down on the chair across from us. "We just need to make Mom cook for us."

Alena listened to Dad's complaints about Mom. She told Dad that she would do something to help. "An agency will help you," she assured Dad.

She crushed out her cigarette in a small ashtray on the coffee table, turned to me and said that she would call an agency. "I don't want to get too involved in these things," she said again. "I've got my own life. But I trust the agencies, so I'll call one that I know. They do counseling and I know they'll help Johnny." Then she whispered to me, "They'll probably find homes for both of you."

Alena didn't stay long. She wanted to get back to her kids. She called the Detroit Children's Center, and arranged for social workers there to talk to our family. Dad couldn't figure out how all this was going to make Mom act better. He told the social workers that they should be talking to Mom instead of calling us all in.

I told the social workers at the JFS about Alena and the Children's Center. The two agencies worked together. Sometimes I was sent to talk to social workers at one agency and sometimes it was the other. They all told me that they wanted to put Johnny and me into foster homes, but it would be hard because of my dad. Michigan law was against us.

Each social worker told me that I would need to go to court. Making a court case would be the only hope we had, they kept telling me. I talked to Mr. Conly several times about going to court. He was a thirty nine year old social worker at the Children's Center. He told me lots of stuff about himself, including things about his family and his two kids. He said that every summer he and his family go on vacations and he taught his kids to swim. I wished he would have adopted me. But instead he kept telling me that my only chance for a good home was to go to court. "We can't do it for you," he kept saying. "The laws don't give us power to help you. You have to be willing to go to court and talk to a judge."

"But what kind of family will he put me in?" I asked.

"That depends on the judge. It will be some family that gets paid from the state to keep you."

"I don't want to live with a family that keeps me only because they are paid to. I want a real family that loves me."

"You're too old to be adopted. People adopt babies. In your case we can try for a foster family where you can live till you're 18."

I looked down. My eyes stuck to the beige throw rug next to my feet.

"What will happen to me after 18?" I asked looking up at him. "How will I live?"

"Don't worry about that," he smiled. "That's a long way off. By then you can take care of yourself."

I looked at him but didn't speak. Then I looked down at my shoes, and the laces that I had tied into tight bows. I didn't want to stay with Mom, but I didn't want to live with strangers that only kept me because they were paid to. I wanted to be a baby so I could be loved and adopted. No one ever loves you once you're grown-up. It was already too late for me.

The social workers wanted me to tell a judge what it was like at home and to say that I wanted to be placed in a foster home. But if I did that, Dad would be mad at me. And what if the foster home wasn't any good? I heard about kids that were abused in foster homes. I wanted to know where I was going before I went. But the social workers wouldn't arrange that. They kept saying that everything depended on the judge. He would decide where I went. I didn't know the judge. What if he didn't like kids? And what if Johnny and I got separated? The social workers couldn't promise that we could stay together. "Don't worry so much," they kept saying. And what about Dad? I knew I would hurt him if I left. He needed a foster home too.

If I were put into a foster home, Mom and Dad wouldn't be my parents anymore. That would be fine not having Mom as my mom. But, I felt sad about Dad. I tried to get used to the idea that Dad wouldn't be my father any more. I stopped calling him Dad. I didn't call him anything when I talked to him. It was really awkward talking to him without addressing him. "Did you see my book?" I called out to the kitchen. Johnny answered, "No! I already told you that!"

"I wasn't talking to you, Johnny, I'm talking to the other person in the kitchen."

I tried to prepare myself for living in a new family, but I constantly worried about it being a mistake. The social workers wouldn't tell me anything. "We don't know," they would say. "It's up to the judge." I was too afraid to go to court.

Several weeks past, Mom had spent all her time resting on the living room couch. But now she was fully rested and loaded with energy for dancing the can-can nonstop, and throwing glasses and knives around the house. I wondered when Dad was going to pick up the phone and call Mom 's sisters and brother, but I didn't ask.

"Call Alena," he said. "Maybe she can do something. Tell her to come right away!"

"O.K," I said. I dialed up Alena. I would rather have her come than Mom's sisters and brother.

"Alena!" I said as she answered the phone, "Dad told me to tell you to come right away because Mom is dancing around the house again and throwing things around."

"OK," she said hesitantly. "I'll be there soon."

Two hours passed and she hadn't come. It was only a twenty minute drive to our house.

"Call Alena again," Dad said.

"O.K." I called again and Alena answered. She told me she was coming. But another hour passed and she still hadn't come. Dad called. She said the same thing to him about coming soon.

Johnny went up to his room. I don't think he said a word all day. Dad and I sat in the living room while Mom danced with all her stored-up energy. Dad looked at Mom as if he were in deep thought. "I wonder why she acts like that," he said. I looked at Dad, but didn't say anything. It was the first time he ever wondered about a reason.

Finally twenty minutes later, Alena came to the door. Dad and I both ran to open the door.

"Why did it take you so long?" I asked before she had a chance to walk in.

She stepped into the living room and stood there. "Well, I know that kids exaggerate. So I thought it wasn't necessary for me to come. But when your father called, I figured I better drag myself over."

"But, Alena! I told you that Dad told me to call you! Why would you think that I exaggerated?"

Dad sat down on a chair near the couch. I continued to stand and look at Alena. She walked over to the couch and flopped down. "Oh, I just know how kids are," she said, as she looked through the living room archway into the dining room where Mom was dancing. I looked at Alena's angry face. I could tell she didn't want to be here, but why couldn't she just say so? Dad looked over to Mom, and his face looked slippery with tears. Alena talked to Dad. Then she got up and tried to talk to Mom. Then she left. Alena couldn't do any more than the rest of us. Dad called her sisters and brother and they came and enjoyed the show for a couple of days till Mom went into the hospital.

A few weeks later, Mom was home again, and spending her time resting on the couch. Alena came by to visit. I answered the door. Johnny was outside somewhere, and Dad wasn't home from work yet. Mom was lying on the couch in a wrinkled house dress. She sat up when Alena walked in and smiled at her. Alena sat next to Mom, crossed her knees and lit a cigarette. I was standing next to Alena but stepped away explaining that I hated cigarette smoke. Alena laughed, "When no one is around, you're probably smoking up a storm."

"No," I said. "I hate cigarette smoke."

"Can't fool me," she said. "I know how kids are. I was smoking at 12."

I looked at the smoke coming out of Alena's mouth. She looked like a dragon-monster in a science fiction movie. I didn't say anything else to Alena. She sat and smoked and chatted away to Mom. Her cigarette smoke turned our house into a gas chamber. When her cigarettes were finished, she left.

A few more weeks passed. Aunt Rebecca called to talk to Mom. I answered the phone and asked about Alena. I hadn't heard from her in the past few weeks.

"She moved to California," Aunt Rebecca said. "She was too busy with her friends to say goodbye."

My hand felt limp around the black receiver, and my glance slid to the floor. I called Mom to the phone and left the room.

*

Several months passed and I continued to talk to social workers at the Children's Center. Different workers kept getting assigned. The first one was a middle-aged man. But each time they switched a social worker it was to someone younger. Then one day when I went in, my young social worker said, "We're closing our case with you. We're sending you back to the Jewish Family Service. They're better trained to work with families."

They sent me back, and I saw Mr. Samuals. I had never seen him before. Both agencies kept changing their people. He was young and according to the date on his diploma on the wall, he had just graduated. It was about my fourth visit with him when he said, "My case load has become very heavy now so I can't see you anymore. I'm sending you back to the Children's Center."

I sat there like a silent rock. New people were more important than I.

I went back to the Children's Center where I was told, "You go back and tell him we already made the agreement that he was to see you. Your case is in his hands!"

I went back and told Mr. Samuals. "You just keep going back!" he said. "They'll see you eventually."

I did go back. The bus stop became my prison. I was trapped there day after day waiting for the bus that kept coming and taking me off to the agencies that kept pushing me away. Neither agency would see me.

Mom had gotten violent again, throwing glasses and dishes at everything and everyone, and dancing the can-can. Johnny tore all my clothes dressing in them. Mom's family came over for the dancing parties, and Dad kept calling Maurie for help. The more Dad called Maurie, the more Maurie talked of killing Johnny. "It will be soon, Jill. Take good care of those moccasins he gave you. It's all you'll have left of him." Maurie, like the rest of Mom's family, had fallen into a sleepwalking dream. His bizarre dream was to kill Johnny. "We've got to get rid of him ," Maurie said.

I breathed hard as panic filled my lungs. I looked at

Maurie. It was like looking at a corpse. He couldn't be revived.

I starved. All my lunch money was being spent on bus fare back and forth to the agencies. The Children's Center told me to go back to Mr. Samuals. Mr. Samuals sent me away. When I phoned him he hung up.

I was in high school, but it would be another few years before Johnny was in high school. This meant we no longer walked home from school together, and I couldn't protect him. Johnny would leave school and run into the alley to hide from other kids. When everyone was gone, he came home. Mom would laugh when Johnny walked in, "We're going to get rid of you, Johnny!" she'd say. Johnny never said anything,

I again called Mr. Samuals for help, but he refused to talk to me. I called the Children's Center, but they told me to see Mr. Samuals.

I went to school looking like a bag lady from the slum. My clothes were torn and had an aura of stink. The girls at school laughed at me. They held their noses as I walked by. My hope of ever being loved was dying. I was dying. I wanted to be in grade school again. I hated high school. I wore bigger ribbons in my hair to make me look younger.

My high school counselor kept telling me to grow up. "Jill!" he'd yell, "you have a D- average! You'll never graduate! The most you'll ever be is a minimum-wage typist, and if you don't start practicing, you won't even be that! Now grow up! Be on your own and forget about your brother!"

I had to save Johnny from Maurie and Mom. If we ran away, we would starve. I didn't have money for food. The only hope was the agencies, but they kept sending me away. My body felt heavy. I hated waking up in the morning. I moved through the day like a lead mannequin. I stopped combing my hair in the morning. It wasn't important what I looked like. Maurie kept trying to find a place where Johnny could be sent, never to return. Finally, Maurie made contact with a rabbi who agreed to send Johnny to an orphanage in Israel.

"He'll be killed there," Maurie kept saying. "Israel is at war. He'll be drafted. He can't even defend himself against the other kids. He'll die on the battle field, and it won't be me who is blamed for murder."

I looked at Maurie with my head so heavy it was hard to move.

Johnny was being sent off to die in a foreign country. He wouldn't know the language. He wouldn't know anyone. But he had a Jewish mother, so a rabbi could send Johnny off to a place where I would never see him again. Maurie brought the papers over for Mom to sign.

"See, we're finally going to get rid of him, once and for all!" Mom laughed.

A place to die, like in a concentration camp. I pictured Johnny on the battlefield covered with blood and crying out to me. I wouldn't be able to save him. I dreamt that Nazis broke into our house and pulled Johnny away from me, and he was gone forever.

The kids at school found Johnny's hiding place in the alley. He kept coming home bloody. The image of Johnny lying dead in desert dust pierced my mind. Each time he walked into the house with his bloody nose, Mom laughed. "You're a freak of nature, Johnny, I can't wait till you die."

I hugged Johnny. "They'll never separate us," I promised. "I'll go with you." He looked at me and smiled. I was his only friend. But I knew there was no way. The paperwork was being made out. Mom and Maurie cheered with the progress of this death certificate. Running away meant death by starvation.

Dad came home from work complaining about being dizzy.

"There must be something you can do to stop Mom and Maurie," I pleaded.

"We can't fight against Mom," he said. "We can't even make her cook for us." He looked weak and tired. "I can hardly stand on my feet," he said. His face was pale. "I almost fainted again at work," he continued. "I'm going to die of a heart attack." He breathed hard and went to his bedroom to lie down.

I worried about Dad. I wondered what I would do if he died. And I still couldn't figure out how to save Johnny. He was black and he didn't fit into his own country. How would he fit in Israel? Would they beat him up there too? I wanted to be with him, but there was no money. There was nowhere to run. We couldn't sleep on the ground in Michigan winter. We were both going to be killed no matter what I did. I pictured the day that he'd be taken away from me. Maurie would be coming to get him and take him off to the airport, and Johnny would look at me wondering why I couldn't save him.

I went to school each day, sat stiffly at my desk as if I were part of it and stared at the clock. The clock didn't move and neither did my eyes. I wanted time and life to end. Each day the teacher spoke but I didn't hear. I stared at the clock, not remembering my thoughts. I awoke for short moments by loud giggles from classmates, "Look at her in her torn clothes, staring at the clock."

I glanced at their laughing faces, and puffy hairdos. My pony tail wasn't combed. I didn't care.

"I have a new dress for Barbara's party," I heard Janet say. They looked back at me and giggled. My eyes went back to the clock, and my mind disappeared.

*

I walked down the street listening to music. I liked the music. It was the tune of *Strangers in the Night*. But the words kept singing *Strange things in my Soup*. There were faces staring at me. I looked at all the faces. Then realized the music was coming from me. I was singing. People on the street were staring at me. The street was unfamiliar and I didn't remember ever being there before. I searched for street signs to tell me where it was that I had wandered.

I managed to get myself to the Jewish Family Service. The receptionist was young like most of the social workers. She wore a freshly ironed dress, high heeled shoes, and perfume that smelled like lilacs.

I looked at my torn blouse. It smelled of sweat. One of Johnny's hairs was on my sleeve. I plucked it off. I looked up at the receptionist.

"My social worker won't see me anymore so I want to see someone else."

"Nope," she said. "I have strict orders from your social worker that if you ever came back, I'm to send you away."

"But they're trying to kill Johnny! I need to see someone!"

She laughed as if she thought I was joking. "You'll have to leave now."

My feet were glued to the floor. My torn blouse smelled of Johnny. I thought of Johnny's bloody nose. She got up from her desk and escorted me to the door.

Chapter 16 - Toilet Paper

I was a corpse. My lifeless body sat through classes day after day, but I wasn't there. I couldn't save Johnny. Memories of the past leeched on to me. I became obsessed with memories of being tortured by Jacoby. I had nightmares about being chased by monsters and people being set on fire. I watched their skin crumble off their bodies. I woke up to the memories of torture.

I had gotten myself from class to class only because my body knew where to take me. The final bell screamed and school ended for the day. My body wandered into the biology lab. I sat down and stared at the clock. Mr. D. walked in from the storage room adjoined to the lab. He startled me because I didn't know anyone was still around.

"What are you doing in here?" he asked.

"Remembering."

"Remembering what?" he asked, as he pulled up a stool and sat next to me.

I looked up at his face trying to decide if I should tell him. He always joked around in class and made funny faces, but now he was looking at me very seriously. He put his hand on my shoulder. "Tell me," he said. "What's been on your mind?"

I looked down at my white bobby socks and my tie shoes. I wasn't wearing Johnny's moccasins because I didn't want to wear them out. I saved those for special occasions. Mr. D. sat there attentively waiting for my answer.

"I remember some stuff my mother did to me." I looked into his face. He was still listening and waiting for me to say more. I nervously rubbed my hands together and bit down on my teeth. The conversation was awkward as I told him in brief and fragmented sentences. I looked away, spoke a sentence, looked at him, rubbed the palm of my hand down the part of my dress that covered my knee, and continued my fragmented sentences. He listened but didn't say very much. Maybe he said two sentences in all the time that we sat there. And we sat there for about an hour. Then he noticed his watch. He looked at me with a sad look on his face. He hadn't made any funny faces. "Jill," he said, "I've got to get home now. Maybe we can talk more some other time." He went over to the small closet in the corner of the lab, grabbed his black leather jacket and put it on. I smiled and almost laughed out loud because that black leather jacket made him look like a motorcycle gang member. Though he probably never even had been on a motor cycle. He waved goodbye and left. I mourned as he walked out. My body became hardened clay with a stiff smile baked on to my face. I continued to sit there and stare at the clock. Finally I got up and wandered down the hall. I stopped at the drinking fountain just outside the girls' lavatory.

"Jill!" I heard someone call out. I turned around.

"Pat, what are you doing still here?"

"I didn't feel like going home," she said. "My parents are fighting over everything. They're even fighting about the divorce that they both want."

"I wish I didn't have to go home, I said. "Do you know any families that might let Johnny and me live with them?"

"No," she said.

"What are you going to do?" I asked. "Are you going to stay here all night?"

"No. I'll go home. But I want some fun first. No one is around. I can have a great time messing things up. Let's go blow up the chem lab again. That was fun."

I took a drink from the water fountain and looked up at the door of the girls room.

"Let's do something different," I said. "Why don't we take toilet paper and decorate the whole school with it."

"Great! Let's get the ass wipe from the girls' room!"

"No." I said. "Let's get it from the boys lavatory. That way they'll think boys did it!"

Pat laughed. "Good thinking, Jill."

We went into every boys lavatory in the building and took every roll of toilet paper. We wrapped it around the principal's desk and threw rolls of toilet paper down the halls like bowling balls down an alley letting the paper unroll as it traveled.

Chapter 17 - The Social Worker

Pat had mentioned something about there being a school social worker. I wasn't really paying attention. She was talking about her parents' divorce and said something about seeing the school social worker. I needed someone and obviously the agencies wouldn't help. I marched myself into my counselor's office. He was sitting behind his desk filling out forms. He was an overweight, impatient old man with gray hair and always dressed in gray suits with an assortment of neckties that looked as though they were strangling his fat neck.

"I hear the school has a social worker," I said. "I want to see her."

He got up and leaned forward with his knuckles on his desk, and looked down at me as if I had just committed some rebellious act. "You don't need her! As soon as you're 16, you'll be old enough to leave home on your own. You can get a job and be an adult."

No, I couldn't. I needed help, and he wouldn't understand. I wanted a family. I didn't want to live alone in some cheap room.

"I'm going to help you," he continued, as he tapped his foot on the floor. "I'm assigning you to more typing classes. By the time you're 16, you'll type well enough to support yourself and be an adult."

He refused to let me see the school social worker, and I was desperate. Pat was in my gym class. I hated gym but now I couldn't wait for gym class so I could talk to her and get more information. At least she might be able to tell me where the social worker's office was. Pat was a husky athletic girl with an addiction to gym. Her whole life was gym. She was one of the few girls at school who didn't make fun of me. All she cared about was gym, not clothes, parties, boys, or even being with other girls. Her world was gym, but lately, that world was being intruded upon by her parents' divorce. Gym hour finally came and there was Pat.

"Pat!" I yelled. "I've been dying to talk to you. I asked my counselor to let me see the social worker, but he said no. Where is her office anyway? And what is she like?"

"I haven't met her," Pat said. "My dad somehow found out that the school had a social worker, and because of the divorce, he got the dumb idea that I needed to see her. But I never went."

"Do you know where her office is? Or how I might see her without permission?"

"Yeah. I have her room number. It's 333A on the third floor. My dad called her and told her that because of family problems he wanted me to see her. So she gave him the room number and told him to send me over. But I never went, and my dad doesn't know that. I've been afraid he'll call her one day and find out that I never went. How about if you go, and you say you're me. Then if my dad checks, I'm in the clear, and you'll be able to see her since that's what you want anyway."

"O.K. But what if we're caught? Did your dad tell her what you look like?"

"Nope. He only asked if it was O.K. for me to come see her and he got the room number. I was by the phone when he called. He only talked for about one minute. And all he said was that we had family problems. He didn't mention the divorce. So you can say what ever you like. You just have to remember that your name is Pat and not Jill."

"O.K., but what if your counselor says something to her and he finds out we traded places?"

"No problem. My counselor is so dumb, he didn't even know there was a school social worker. My dad talked to my counselor once and my counselor said that the school didn't have such a service. I'm not sure how my dad finally found out about the social worker. But he doesn't have any contact with my counselor, and now my dad thinks my counselor is a jerk anyway. And for sure my counselor won't say anything to the social worker, because he doesn't know she exists."

"O.K room 333A."

I searched the entire third floor till I found her office. It was a tiny closet- sized room with her name above the door - Miss Parker. There was a small window in the upper part of the door. I stood on my tip toes and looked in. She was an old lady with a friendly smile and white frizzy permed hair with a blue tinge to it. She was sitting in her office smoking cigarettes and reading magazines. There was a large stack of magazines in the left corner of the room. On her desk there was a large glass ashtray filled with ashes and butts. How lucky that I found her and she wasn't busy. I walked into her office and told her that I was Pat. She smiled and crushed out her cigarette in her glass ashtray, spilling some of the ashes on the desk. She looked happy to see me, as if I were an old friend. She got up and hugged me. She was warm and acted just like I'd want a mother to act. I told her about me, and she told me about her and her sister Helen. The two of them never married and had always lived together. We chatted for about an hour when the bell rang and I had to go to class.

I came back the next day. She told me how she and her sister spend their weekends at their cottage, and she invited me to come with them. I told her I couldn't. I would not go anywhere unless I could take Johnny with me, and she didn't want Johnny.

"Just us girls," she said.

"No." I said. Besides, it didn't seem like it would be too much fun with two old ladies, and no other kids around.

It was fun pretending to be Pat. Each day in gym class, I told Pat about how well our impostor game was going. It was fun for both of us.

I didn't really like Miss Parker that well, because sitting around with her in her smoky little closet and listening to her talk about her and her sister Helen and their cottage, wasn't that much fun or helpful. But at least she was someone to pay attention to me. I knew that there was someone who looked forward to seeing me each day. She hugged me each time I came into her office. I liked having someone pay attention to me, though I hated the cigarette smell that was on her breath, hair, clothes, and all around her. Walking into her office was like walking into a burning chimney.

One day about a month later, my counselor called me into his office to yell at me for skipping English class. I hated English class. I simply didn't care how many times Lady MacBeth washed her hands. But of all the times for my counselor to call me into his office. It was right at the time I was supposed to be seeing Miss Parker, and I couldn't tell him that I had to leave. I was stuck.

When my counselor finally finished yelling at me, I went up to the third floor and was about to go to Miss Parker's office, when Pat came running up to me.

"What happened!? Where were you?" she shouted.

"I've just been released from my counselor's torture chamber," I explained. "What happened that you're here?"

"When you didn't show up, she went to my study hall to look for me. She asked the teacher if he knew where I was and the teacher pointed at me! She looked at me and insisted that I wasn't Pat. The teacher kept insisting that I was Pat, and all the kids laughed at her as if she were senile. When she asked me who I was, I told her my name was Jill. But everyone laughed and the teacher got angry, and they finally figured out what happened. Now I'm in trouble because she said I have to start seeing her too. She said she wants to see both of us."

Miss Parker came out to the hall. She said she would continue to see both of us at the same time. So Pat and I kept going every day to see her. Miss Parker still sometimes goofed and called me Pat. But at least she didn't tell my counselor what happened or Pat's counselor. So now Pat too had to endure the smoky little closet. Every time Miss Parker turned her head to light a cigarette, or look around the room, Pat would stick her tongue out at Miss Parker. One time Miss Parker bent down to pick up a magazine, and Pat kicked her in the butt, missing Miss Parker by an inch. Pat and I both laughed, and Miss Parker never did know why. The Bitch is what Pat called her behind her back. Pat was bored listening to Miss Parker talk about her and her sister and the cottage in the open air, while we sat in a smoky room and choked. Miss Parker didn't seem to like Pat much either. She never invited Pat to the cottage, only me. She kept insisting that it would be good for me to go there.

"We're going again this weekend," she said. "We'll leave Friday right after school. How about coming with us?"

"No. Besides, this Friday, my mother will be coming home from one of her trips to the mental hospital."

"Oh, but it will be fun having you at the cottage with us," she said.

"No. I don't want to go," I insisted.

On Friday, she told me that it would be good for me to take a break and go with her and her sister to their cottage. As she looked at me and talked, Pat made faces at her. It was hard for me not to laugh. I kept my face straight and told her again that I wouldn't go anywhere without Johnny, and I reminded her that tonight was the night Mom was coming back.

"But we'd love to have you with us."

"No." I said

She pressed her lips together and slammed her hand on the table.

Later that evening my mother came home. With Dad's help, she unpacked her clothes and several bottles of tranquilizers. Her hair was neatly combed, and her dress looked as though it had been ironed. Johnny and I were watching T.V. when I heard the phone ring and Mom pick it up.

"Who are you?" I heard Mom say. "Miss Parker...no, I didn't."

I walked slowly to the phone to hear more. Mom slammed down the phone and glared at me.

"You whore! The school social worker just called to tell me that you're a whore! I'll fix you."

"Come on," Dad pleaded. "Just unpack your things and forget about it."

"Forget about it!?"

"Yeah, people are always talking and making trouble. Just unpack and forget about it."

I slowly turned away and went back to Johnny who was still hypnotized by the T.V.

"I'll fix that Jill," I heard Mom scream.

I didn't sleep all night. I thought Miss Parker was trying to help me. Why would she call Mom? Sure she was angry that I wouldn't go to her cottage, but how could she do this to me? I looked at the clock in my bedroom every 15 minutes. I couldn't wait till Monday, so I could tell my counselor about this. Monday seemed an eternity away.

I spent most of the weekend outside with Johnny. Mom and Dad were busy cleaning the house. I did manage to call Pat and tell her what happened. She said she wasn't going to see Miss Parker anymore anyway because her father finally decided Miss Parker wasn't helping. He was especially angry when Pat explained to him that she never talked to Miss Parker alone, but always with me. Her father thought that was a strange way to counsel someone.

When Monday finally came, I stormed into my counselor's office and without sitting down or taking time to catch my breath I told him what happened.

He slammed his fist on his desk and stood up. "Serves you right!" he yelled. "I told you not to see her! I tried to protect you from that nutty lesbian." His face reddened. "Why do you think that with all the troubled kids in this school, she spends her time only reading magazines? None of the counselors send students to her! I told you once and I'll tell you again, study your typing and grow up!"

I didn't want to drop out of school at 16 and be an adult. I stood in front of him, looking at his angry face and clenched fist and tried to figure out how to explain.

"There's no chance for you ever to go to college with your grades!" he continued. "Typing is the only chance for a job you'll ever get!"

I'd rather die than be forced to give my life away as a minimum wage typist. I'd never make enough money to support both Johnny and me.

"But for now," he continued, "you're suspended for the rest of the week. Now get out! Sneaking behind my back to the nutty lesbian! I'll teach you. You were just looking for trouble! And, since you thought it was going to be so much fun to see that old les, I'm going to arrange for you to keep seeing her. You'll see her once a week! Now get out!!"

I put the hood of my black parka over my head and sat outside in the school parking lot all day. I was wordless. I don't know why he thought I was "just looking for trouble." It was as if he thought I knew that there was something wrong with her and that's why I wanted to see her. It was so hard for me to speak out. I felt as if I had a rag stuffed in my mouth. I wanted to tell him about the agencies and explain that I had no one. But I was so used to not speaking that I couldn't talk to save myself. It was senseless to explain anything to Mom or Dad, and now I had a hard time explaining anything to anyone. I sat outside and felt happy and sad at the same time. The fact that my counselor had now let me know that something was wrong with Miss Parker gave me a sense of relief. She was at fault; not me. Yet, I felt a sad helplessness. It was as if a tree had fallen on me and I was trapped under it. He had a daughter my age who gave him a lot of problems. She was eager to grow up and wore make-up and high heeled shoes whenever she thought her father wouldn't catch her. He was angry at her for trying to grow up too soon, and angry at me for not wanting to grow up. Every time I told him how I was afraid to grow up, he treated me as if I were deliberately being a brat. He didn't believe me. He seemed to think all teenagers were like his daughter. She couldn't wait till she was out on her own. I felt angry at Mr. A. I knew he would never want his daughter to leave home at sixteen and support herself. Yet it was O.K. for me.

I remember the first time I met Mr. A. All freshmen had to attend an orientation meeting with their counselor.

I found out later from other kids with other counselors that the purpose of the meeting was to get to know our counselor. He was supposed to tell us that if we ever had a problem, we were supposed to go to him. But our orientation meeting wasn't that way. He lectured to us about what it was going to be like in high school. He read off some statistics. He told us what percentage of us would go to college, what percentage would drop out, what percentage would get pregnant and a few other percentages that I don't remember and wasn't paying attention to anyway. Then he told us about how he wanted to be a doctor but he had flunked out of school. Being a doctor was his life long dream and his dream crumbled. As he spoke, I felt sorry for him. I got the strong feeling that he really didn't like being a school counselor, especially when he mentioned his daughter and how hard it was to deal with her. I got the clear impression that he thought being a doctor would have been a lot easier. At the end of his lecture, he told us all to study hard so we could be what ever we wanted. He never did mention anything about coming to him if we had problems.

I continued to sit outside and at 4:00 I saw Mr. D. leave the building and head for his car. He was one of the very few people I liked. He was friendly, smiled a lot, told jokes in class, and always let me talk to him. I told my math teacher once that my mother was taken to the hospital, and before I could finish my sentence she said, "I don't want to hear about it. My sister is in critical condition in a hospital and I don't want to hear anyone else's problems." At least Mr. D. let me finish my sentences. I ran up to him.

"Why didn't you show up for class?" he asked.

I told him about my suspension. He wasn't surprised. He told me something about the teacher's union and the school superintendent that everyone hated. All that had something to do with why they couldn't fire Miss Parker. I was too upset to listen to everything he said, so I still can't figure out why the teacher's union and the superintendent wouldn't get rid of her. He also said that the Detroit school district was the poorest paying, so it was hard to find good staff in the first place.

Mr. D. had to get home. He said we could talk more after my suspension was over. He got into his car and I watched him drive away.

I started walking home. I just wanted help, I wanted a family to live with. I didn't want to have to grow up and live alone somewhere. I wanted to be saved from Mom. Those hospitals never seemed to help her. They never kept her long enough. It's against the law in Michigan to keep someone in an institution all of his or her life. People can't be held against their will for very long. So, Mom always came back.

Mom learned early that to be crazy meant to be powerful. It meant she could get away with things that normal people couldn't. If she wanted to return a dress to a store where the merchandise was not returnable, all she needed to do was throw things around and scream. She jumped up on counters and shouted, "I'm a mental patient! I must have my way!" Horrified sales clerks gave her whatever she wanted. When we got home, she'd laugh at what she got away with.

When I was 6 months old, my father was drafted. It was World War II. Dad left for the military and Mom was left with a new baby. She threw a temper tantrum. She threw knives. She screamed. Neighbors called relatives. Relatives called the Red Cross. The Red Cross sent Dad home. Mom had power over the military. She got them to send Dad back.

Mom was sent to the mental hospital for a couple weeks. Just long enough to get tranquilized. She was always sent home even though it was known to everyone that she was unfit and unready. There was no money to keep her longer. And, as years passed, Michigan laws tightened against us. It became hard to get her committed even when she was in a violent rage. The law was like a pendulum that swung from one extreme to another. There was a famous case where a woman gave birth to a son while she was in the mental hospital. The son was kept in the hospital so he could be with his mother. Years passed. Mother and son stayed. Staff changed. Nurses and orderlies and doctors came and went.

The mother died. The young boy still stayed. The staff saw that the boy could not read or write. Everyone assumed he was retarded. He became 10, 11, 12, then a teenager. He still could not read or write. It was obvious to everyone that he was retarded. When the boy was in his 40's, a new director was appointed. The new director ordered that all the patients be tested to see what was wrong with them. The tests showed that the boy - who was now a man- had normal intelligence and normal mental functioning. Nothing was wrong with him. He could not read or write because no one ever taught him. No one ever gave him a book. He was there because he was born there. It was because of that scandal that Michigan law changed. No one could any longer, be held against his or her will. The pendulum was now at the other extreme. So, even though everyone knew that my mother was unfit and even dangerous, it was a long procedure just to get her committed, and then, she could not be kept for very long. She learned that all she had to do was demand that she be released and she was freed. She had power over the system. She could come home.

Chapter 18 - Getting Close

Months passed. I was a prisoner waiting for execution day. There were some legal problems prolonging Johnny's fate of being sent away forever. Meanwhile, Mom had been in and out of the hospital again, and I kept waking up several times during the nights with dreams of people being burned to death. Night was a refuge for day, but nowhere was there refuge for night. One man in my dreams fell into a huge industrial vat of acid. His skin turned black and peeled off. I felt a sensation of falling from a far distance. I dreamt I was on an elevator in a tall building and the cable snapped. I smashed. The fall knocked me out of my sleep. I looked up and watched the clock. Several hours passed.

I had become a rag doll that dragged itself around through each day. My high school counselor forced me to continue seeing Miss Parker once a week. Sometimes I saw her alone and sometimes there would be one or two other kids up there too. All she ever did was lecture us. She talked about how she and her sister Helen had spent their lives together. The two of them were experts in knowing about love. They were each other's support in good and bad times. I kept looking up at the clock through the clouds of cigarette smoke. She spent most of her work day sitting alone in her office enjoying her smoky room. At least she didn't call my house anymore. It seemed the only kids who ever saw her had parents who were too consumed with themselves to care or notice what was happening to their kids. I remember one girl coming into Miss Parker's office and crying about her father sexually abusing her. Miss Parker lectured the girl about the importance of being obedient. I don't know what happened to that girl. I never saw her again.

Then there was one case that was really funny. It had to do with Esther, a boy-crazy classmate of mine. She always came to school in tight skirts and sweaters, and made her body wiggle when she walked. She wanted to go into the military right after high school graduation, because she had a thing about military men being sexy, and thought that joining the military was going to be one big orgy. Her parents were always nagging her to do better in school. They wanted her to be a school teacher. Esther hated school. She had some pretty big conflicts with her parents and as a result her parents arranged for her to see Miss Parker. Miss Parker tried to convince Esther that she was a lesbian. For some reason, Miss Parker even wrote down on Esther's school records that Esther was a lesbian. Esther screamed bloody murder to her parents and tried to get her parents to file a complaint against Miss Parker. But Esther's parents refused. They considered it a blessing because now the military wouldn't accept Esther.

Meanwhile, I kept Pat informed about all the crazy things Miss Parker was doing. Pat and I had a special name for Miss Parker. We had searched through several dictionaries to find the right word for her. We decided to call her the "Zona". We liked the sound of the word zona. In Hebrew it means whore, and in English it is the name of a skin disease. The zona gave problems to every kid she saw. Indeed, she was a disease.

Pat was the only friend I had. It was hard on me when she graduated and went off to college. Pat wasn't concerned about growing up and being alone. For me it was a curse.

I stood in front of the mirror in the locker room and gently tugged my pony tail. The face in the mirror looked too old, and I wondered what I could do to look younger. If I were younger, someone might care about me. Mr. D. had two little kids. If I were their age, maybe he'd adopt me. The girls next to me were putting on lipstick and trying to look older.

"Wait till you see the new dress I'm wearing to Nancy's party," Jan said to Alice as they both smeared on Dracula blood-colored lipstick. Jan pointed at me and giggled like a hyena. "Look at the ribbon in her hair. What a baby! I bet she'll be 25 before her parents let her use lipstick."

"Yeh," Alice shouted out to everyone. "I bet she'll be 30 before her parents let her wear a bra."

The entire pack of locker room hyenas exploded into laughter. My eyes looked straight into the mirror as I pretended not to notice them. I stroked my pony tail, then retied my ribbon. The hysterical hyenas pointed their paws at me, and thundering laughter echoed off the walls. The bell rang. The pack ran off.

I stood there looking into the mirror. Gym was my last class of the day. It was now time for me to go home. My rag-doll body sank in sadness. I was being tossed back and forth between school and home, between hyenas and snakes.

I dragged myself home and wandered around toward the back door, then just stood there looking up at the sky. It looked so far away. The farther out I looked the smaller I felt. Anyone looking down on me from such a high distance wouldn't even notice me. I would be just another blade of grass. I swung my head back down to the ground and entered the back door. I kicked off my boots and hung my coat in the back closet. Maurie's voice was coming from the living room. He often came over to discuss Johnny and Israel with Mom. They had found an orphanage in Israel that would accept Johnny. There were only a few small details that still had to be worked out. My hope that the whole thing would all fall through was gone.

I walked into the living room. Mom sat starry eyed on the couch, hair in bobby pins and face smirked as Maurie sat next to her and talked.

"The rabbi has connections there," he said. "It's going to work."

Mom kissed Maurie on the cheek, and his face blossomed into a smile. I dragged myself past the two of them and headed towards the stairs.

Maurie turned his head to me. "Jill, it looks like it's going through. Save your moccasins. We'll probably be getting rid of him in a month."

I pushed myself up the stairs and into my bedroom, then flopped down on my bed and waited. My whole life was being spent waiting; waiting for morning so I could go to school and then waiting at school so I could go home.

"There's fatso!" I heard Mom shout out the window to someone.

"Mom! Don't act like that!" Maurie pleaded. "Why can't you be like other mothers? Why can't you be friendly to neighbors?"

I could hear from the tone of Maurie's voice that his happiness had turned to tears.

"Mom, I keep doing so much for you. Why can't you act nice?"

There were a few seconds of silence, then I heard Maurie thunder, "I hate Dad! He's the one who gives you all this trouble and makes you act bad!"

I wanted to tell Maurie that he's the one acting bad. But, it did no good to tell Maurie anything. All he would do is explode into anger and start blaming me.

The front door slammed. It was the Maurie slam. At least he was gone. I waited. The rag doll on my bed waited. I remembered myself as a preschooler waiting for Mom. I thought about all the times Mom took me downtown to the City County Building. It was a huge gray building with lots of steps leading to the doors. At the bottom of all those steps were two cement flower tubs, one on each side of the steps and each one contained a small tree. "Just sit here on the steps," she would say. "I'll be right back." Noon came and the sun was overhead. I starved. People hurried in and out of the building while I quietly sat and waited. The sun moved. I wanted food. I asked a lady to help me find my mommy. She told me to wait. She said she was sure my mom would be back soon. I asked a young boy to help me find my mommy. He said that no one could help me because no one knew what my mother looked like. I waited, and occasionally went inside the big building to use the bathroom. Then I hurried out, but Mom wasn't there. The sun disappeared. Mom finally came.

I sat on my bed waiting. I boiled like a geyser but appeared frozen like a glacier. There was a sound at the front door. It was a Johnny sound. "Hi Mom," I heard him say.

"We're getting rid of you, Johnny!" she yelled. "You're a freak, Johnny! You're a freak!"

I walked to the stairway to call Johnny upstairs, but he was already on his way up. He kept his eyes on the stairs as he walked. He walked like a prisoner approaching the firing squad.

"It will be O.K." I tried to reassure him. He walked over to his room as I stood at the top of the stairway watching him. He had a couple scratches on his face, and his jacket had a small rip along the seam of the shoulder. I knew the kids at school had attacked him. He kept his eyes to the floor and entered his room. I stood in empty silence.

I heard Dad's car pull up from work. I went downstairs to meet him. He was in the kitchen looking at the stove. "Look at this,." he said. "No dinner. I give her money enough for food, and there's nothing!"

"Dad, we have to do something to help Johnny."

"We can't control Mom," he answered. "Look at this! I work hard for her in the factory and this is how she treats me.

I thought when I married her that I would have someone to take care of me. I never had a mother. I never had nobody. When my father and us kids came to this country, I had to go out and work. I didn't have no chances to go to school and learn good English. People made fun of me. "Greenhorn," they called me. "There's the Polish greenhorn," they'd say. He stared down at the floor, then wiped his nose with his palm. "I worked hard all of my life. I was 16 when I came here. I got myself a job and an old car to get me back and forth. Your mother lived on our block and liked me. She came to my work place and hung around my car all day waiting for me to get off work. I thought she loved me." He took his hanky out of his pocket, blew his nose and continued. "She had dropped out of high school and everyday from early morning she sat in my car waiting for me. All day long she sat there, stretched out in my back seat, waiting just for me. Who ever thought it would end up like this!" He blotted some tears off his face. "I was so dizzy again today in the factory that I almost passed out. I felt my heart racing. You wait and see. I'll die of a heart attack. Then she'll be sorry." He smeared his face with his hanky. "I'm dizzy, Jill. I can tell I'm going to die. She'll be sorry. Then they'll be no money for food. She can't pay for this house without me, either. She'll be out on the street." He put his hands on his forehead. "I can't stand up, Jill. I'm dizzy."

"Dad, tell Maurie to leave Johnny alone! You're the father in the house!"

I stood there like a mourner. He stumbled past me toward his room, and lay down like a corpse. If he died, I too would be out on the streets. I leaned against the kitchen sink and waited.

"Come on, Sis," I heard Johnny say as he entered the kitchen. "Where's the peanut butter? Let's eat."

"Sure Johnny," I said, "It will be OK. " I grabbed some bread and we made sandwiches. We ate in silence.

Each morning, I pushed myself off to school where I watched the clock and waited for time to die so I could go home and sleep. Sleep was the only place to hide. Morning kept interrupting my sleep and outside into knee-high snow I would make my path to school.

My bare legs were cold. In spite of all those years of freezing cold, the Detroit School Board insisted that girls wear dresses to school. The style for girls was ankle socks, and ankle boots. The rest of our legs were naked. Our dresses and coats dangled around our knees as the wind and snow scraped our legs. Boys could wear long underwear under wool slacks, but girls had to wear dresses to look like little ladies. It wasn't ladylike for us to cover our legs, but it was ladylike to go bare legged.

Even in grade school I complained about it. I complained to my home room teacher, Mrs. Mc Grathe. "Why can't girls wear warm slacks like the boys?" I asked. "Why do we have to wear dresses and go bare legged? My legs are cold and my whole body shivers."

She laughed. "Women have been dressing this way for hundreds of years,." she said. "Why should we change?"

"But we've had cannibalism for thousands of' years," I protested. "And we changed!"

She looked at me and laughed. Then she went back to grading the papers on her desk.

My gym teacher, Mr. K was just as bad. I remember him standing in the playground at recess watching over us. We all had to go out at recess even though it was below zero. The boys played together and the girls huddled against the building shivering. We spent recess squatting down trying to cover our legs with our coats. I went up to Mr. K. My legs were red and looked like raw hamburger from the snow rubbing against them with each step. I looked up at him. "Why don't you allow girls to wear slacks so we can keep warm? Or at least let us stay inside at recess.?" He laughed. "Girls have more body fat than men. They can take this weather."

He was a fat man in wool slacks over long underwear that showed every time he'd slip his thick boots on or off. "Besides," he said, "girls don't look good in slacks."

I kept walking and finally reached the high school and went to my locker. I thought about Miss Parker being paid to sit on the third floor in her little office smoking cigarettes and reading magazines. I thought of Johnny. Mom and Maurie wanted him dead. I thought of Jacoby. I leaned against the wall and slid to the floor. I felt heavy. I couldn't get up. The bell rang. It rang again. An hour must have passed. I picked myself up, took my coat off and put it into my locker. I went up to the biology lab. There was a class in there. It wasn't my class but I walked in anyway and sat at the back of the room. Mr. D. was explaining something to the class. Something about frogs. He saw me and knew I didn't belong there, but he didn't say anything.

Chapter 19 - Telling Johnny

I wandered home after school, my skin burned in the icy air. Everything was covered with snow. No matter where I looked there was blinding white. I listened to the crunchy sound of snow under my feet as I forced myself forward.

How was I going to prepare Johnny for the day when Maurie would send him away to Israel, and I couldn't go with him? I pictured him at the airport boarding the plane and looking back at me, waiting for me to board with him, but I wouldn't. I would only stand there like a rock watching him and the plane disappear. I kept having dreams that he was frantically searching for me. He looked everywhere but couldn't find me. I wanted to tell him where I was. I wanted to reach out to him, but I was trapped under some bushes where he couldn't see or hear me.

I thought about the moccasins. That would be all that was left of my brother. I had been telling Johnny that it would be O.K., that they could never separate us. But now I needed to warn him. Slowly, I walked into the house through the back door. I pulled off my boots and brushed off the snow, then hung my coat in the hall closet.

Mom was sleeping on the couch. Her face was lifeless but her stomach moved up and down as she breathed. Her mouth was slightly opened. She was a vicious zoo animal asleep in the living room. I slipped past her and sneaked upstairs towards Johnny's room. It would be cruel not to warn him.

"Johnny," I called out to him as I approached his opened door. He sat on the edge of his bed, still and silent, his head bent staring at the floor. He too had become a mannequin.

"Johnny," I said again. He stood up. His large brown eyes looked at me and he smiled. He became alive.

"I've been waiting for you to come home, Jill. At least we'll always be together." He moved his arms out toward me.

I stood as if glued to the floor. I breathed in slowly. My body stiffened like wood." I have bad news for you," I said.

His eyes fixed themselves on me. His face didn't move.

"I have something to tell you, Johnny. Are you ready?" He didn't move. "I can't go with you. I'll be staying here."

His face looked numb. It was the face of a mannequin. He didn't speak.

"I don 't have the money to go with you. It will be a long time. I'll need to get a job and make some money. But first, I'll have to finish school. It will be a long time, Johnny." I stood there for a while, then left the room.

Chapter 20 - Boarding School

My mind was a tug of war. My thoughts pulled back and forth between Johnny and Jacoby. I kept wishing I were a small kid who could be adopted. I wished Mr. D. would adopt me. Then I'd think of Jacoby and pace. Memories of him gushed into my mind. My legs walked in desperate steps, but I never arrived anywhere. My fists clenched.

Mom was vacuuming the rug. I walked into the room and watched her. I hated the rug because it let her stand on it. She finished, pulled out the plug and started wrapping the cord around the trunk of the cleaner. She looked up at me.

"Mom, how did you meet Jacoby?"

She smiled, her eyes gazing, she didn't answer. "Mom, how did you meet Jacoby?"

She laughed and slipped her hand under the elastic band of her slacks and scratched her crotch. "It's not my fault," she chuckled with starry eyes. "He did it. I didn't do anything." She pulled her hand out of her crotch and put the vacuum away. I was never able to get a straight answer from her. That question was to plague me the rest of my life.

I went to my room and decided to wash out my green sweater. I picked it up, paced around my room, looked at it, got some soap, paced around, and finally several hours later, I finished washing my sweater. I felt confused. I didn't understand why so much time had passed.

I kept picturing myself being dragged to the guillotine. My head, chopped off, and finally, nothingness.

I don't remember how much time passed. Maybe weeks, maybe a couple of months, I walked into the house. I don't remember where I was coming from. Johnny was in the living room, sitting silently and motionless. I smiled at him. He didn't say anything. His hands were folded together in his lap, and his head was bent toward the floor. I could hear Mom in the kitchen washing dishes. She threw one on the floor, and I heard the smashing of many pieces. I ran into the kitchen.

"It didn't work," she said. "Johnny can't go to Israel. It fell through!"

I ran back into the living room where Johnny was still sitting. "Johnny!" I exclaimed. "She said you're not going!" Johnny sat motionless as if he were one of the stuffed pillows on the couch. Not even a move of an eye. The expression on his face looked as if it were painted on. "Johnny, what happened? Did you know you weren't going?" He nodded his head yes.

"Why didn't you tell me?" He didn't answer. I think he thought that I wouldn't care. I had already told him, I wouldn't go with him. I had already said I would finish school instead of working to get the money. I sat down on the couch next to Johnny and hugged him. It was the first time in a long time that I hugged him. Till now I had only stood next to him. To reach out and touch him had been too painful. I was about to lose him. I couldn't stand to touch someone that I was about to lose forever. He was being sent off to be killed. I couldn't touch him.

I never did find out what happened. Mom never gave straight answers. Maurie stopped coming over, and Dad was too busy living in the past, and mumbling about the nothing he never had. Whenever I looked at him, it seemed as if he were in a trance.

"Dad," I'd say.

"I'm tired," he'd answer. "I can't stand Mom's brother."

"Dad," I'd say.

"I want to watch T.V." he'd answer. "I'm tired. I can't stand up. I never had anything from anyone."

Talking to Dad was like talking to a tape recording. It can't hear. It isn't aware. Yet, it can talk. It says the same words over and over again.

Then one Saturday I was home watching T.V. Dad was at work. Johnny was outside. Mom picked up the phone by the sink and started dialing, "I need the police," she said. "My son, Johnny, just tried to kill me!"

I shut off the T.V. She gave our address, spelled out Johnny's name and hung up. She stayed in the kitchen. I stayed in the living room and sat in a chair in the corner. Two policemen came to the door. Mom walked past me as if she didn't see me and answered the door. "He tried to kill me," she said. "Here, let me show you the kitchen chair."

The two policemen walked past me and followed Mom to the kitchen. "See," she said.

"The leg of this chair is loose! It's proof he tried to kill me! Now get rid of him!"

I walked over to the kitchen doorway. The police looked confused. They looked at Mom as if to look for injuries, but all that showed was her gazing eyes, and her day-dreamy smile. The police looked around the room. I stood there like a piece of furniture. I hoped that they would ask me what happened, but they ignored me. The two officers looked alike. Two tall men in blue suits. The younger one looked up at the ceiling. I glanced up there too wondering what he was looking for. Then he looked at Mom and his eyes stared into hers as if he had never seen eyes before. There was silence. The older cop was writing something on the clipboard and the younger one turned to him and asked, "How do we handle this? Maybe we should just leave."

"No." answered the older one. "Let's write this up. This was a call for us to investigate, so let's give this over to a judge for juvenile court."

"O.K.," the younger one said. Mom stood there smiling, and her eyes were gazing out at something, but I don't know what. The two officers scribbled something on a clipboard. "You'll get a notice for a court date," the older one said to Mom. Then they walked past me again as if I weren't there. I wished they would have asked me questions. It would take a question to me to break the inertia of my silence. The two men left. I went back to the living room and sat.

I didn't say anything, not even to Johnny when he came into the house later. Johnny sat next to me and we both watched T.V. When Dad came home from work, Mom was still in the kitchen. Dad walked into the house and straight to the kitchen. I think he noticed Johnny and me watching T.V. I got up and walked over to the kitchen door. Mom was sweeping the floor. She looked up at Dad and said, "There's going to be a court date. You can talk to a judge."

"Good!" Dad said. "I'll tell him! No one ever gave me anything. I'll tell him. I was a good kid all my life. I lost my mother. I never took anything from anyone. My mother shouldn't have been taken. I'll tell him!"

Dad went to the stove to see if there was any food cooking. There was a pot of spaghetti. "Let's eat," he said. He must have noticed me standing there because he didn't say anything to me. "Johnny," he yelled. "Come eat."

Several days passed. I hardly spoke. I came and went from school. I remembered the scene in *A Tale of Two Cities* where two people were in a truck being driven to the guillotine. It was me. In my mind, I waited for the guillotine.

The notice came and stated that Johnny and his parents were to go before Judge Lincoln in the Juvenile Court. There was no mention of me in the notice, but I would follow along anyway.

"We go to court Thursday at 4:00," Mom said to Dad.

"Good, " Dad answered. "I'll tell him!"

Johnny didn't ask questions and I didn't speak. I had so much to say, but I had become a silent observer. Thursday came and we all got into Dad's blue Ford and drove toward the court house. Surely, Johnny must have wondered what was going on. He just came quietly like a handcuffed prisoner. I couldn't explain or speak unless I were asked. My voice was paralyzed but my body was in a state of anxiety where all I could do was pace around in silence and go nowhere.

We entered the court house and Mom started looking for room 5A. The directory on the wall showed us which way to go. We went down a long pale yellow hallway, then a black arrow pointed to the right. Then there was room 5A. We all walked in. It was a large room with lots of wooden folding chairs all set up as if the room were prepared for a large group of people. But all that was there were the same two policemen. They were talking to a fortyish looking man in a business suit who was sitting at a large desk in front of the room. There was a pile of papers on the desk and the man in the suit was reading the clipboard as he talked with the two policemen. Mom and Dad walked in first and Johnny and I followed. I was trying to decide which chair to sit on when Dad yelled out to the judge. "No body ever gave me anything. I was a good kid all my life!"

The man looked puzzled. I assumed he was the judge, though he hadn't even introduced himself yet. The two policemen nodded at the judge. The judge looked at the clipboard, and then at Dad.

"I never did anything wrong!" Dad said. "I didn't have a mother. I never did anything bad!"

The judge looked at the older policeman who nodded as if

to say, "yes." Then the judge looked at Johnny and then Mom, then at Dad.

"I never did anything, I tell you!" Dad shouted.

"Do you know why you're here?" asked the judge as he stared at Dad. "Do you know the purpose?"

"Purpose?" Dad asked. Now Dad looked puzzled. I wanted to tell Dad, but he didn't ask. .

Mom smiled and I could tell from her eyes she was day-dreaming. I never knew what she was dreaming about. Johnny sat down in one of those wooden folding chairs and looked down towards his shoes. I kept wondering if Johnny knew why we were there. I looked around the room. An empty room of chairs and a judge at the front. It looked like a funeral parlor. The judge was waiting for the mourners before making the eulogy.

"Is this your son?" asked the judge to Mom and Dad.

"Yes," said Dad, still standing with a confused expression stuck on his face. Then Dad turned to Johnny and yelled, "Stand up!"

"No, I don't feel like it," Johnny mumbled.

I was still standing. I hadn't decided which one of the many chairs to sit on. It took me a long time to even make small decisions.

"Get up!" Dad yelled again. Johnny didn't move. He didn't even turn his head.

"See, judge," Dad said. "Nobody gave me nothing! I never took anything! I was a good kid all my life!"

Dad turned his head toward Johnny. "Get up!" Dad demanded.

"No!" Johnny yelled back without moving.

"You two don 't seem to get along well," the judge remarked. He looked at Johnny then at Dad, then at Mom. I felt invisible. He looked back at Dad, "Do you have any idea why you're here?" he asked Dad

"I never took anything in my life!" Dad screamed back. The judge looked more puzzled than Dad. There was silence. I looked around the room at the silent chairs.

"Well," the judge finally said, "I think what I'll do, since this is a court case, is we'll make Johnny a ward of the court and find a place for him to live." The judge explained that he knew of a couple boarding schools, and that the state would pay all Johnny's expenses.

"I never had anything," answered Dad.

"He's from Europe," Mom explained.

"O.K.," said the judge, 'We'll be getting back to you."

I stood there trying to decide what chair to sit on, and what I should say or do. I was stuck because no one asked me anything. I wished the judge would have talked to me. I wished the judge would have sent Dad to a shrink for help. But the judge's only concern was where to put Johnny.

"I never took anything," Dad yelled as we all left the room. Dad was some kind of parrot with a limited vocabulary. I had asked him several times to go get help from a shrink or an agency. The Agencies pushed me away, but I thought that maybe because he was a man, they might help him. He was in so much pain about not having a mother. Whenever, I mentioned to Dad about getting help, he always answered, "How can just talking do any good?"

"I don't know. But try anyway!" I 'd tell him.

"It won't do any good," he'd say. "We need to make Mom act better, that's all."

My words never seemed to get through to Dad. Talking to Mom was senseless, and now I simply could not talk unless someone pried and no one pried. I could go through a whole day on just a few "HI's" or a no, or a yes. My words were useless.

Johnny was sent to a school in Michigan. At least it wasn't Israel. At least the school wasn't at war. At least he was somewhere safe.

I thought about those social workers that I had seen at the two agencies. They told me they couldn't rescue Johnny and me because they needed Dad's permission to place us anywhere. Why didn't they tell me to call the police?

I was alone. Alone with Mom and Dad. My high school counselor couldn't understand my attachment to a black brother. "Forget about him!" he snapped. "Leave school! Go get a job and leave home!"

Chapter 21 - It's Over

Johnny seemed happy at that school. It was a special school for kids who came from messed up families. He got to see a shrink up there, and we visited him every few weeks. Dad never did ask why Johnny was sent there. I felt happy that Johnny was in a safe place. Mr. D even drove me up to see Johnny once, and sometimes I would baby-sit for Mr. D's kids. I started combing my hair, and now I also had clean clothes.

It was my senior year; I had signed up for some science classes and went into my counselor's office to get his signature on my new schedule.

"Oh, no you don't!" he yelled. "You're just trying to get my goat with your disobedience! Each one of those classes requires a second and third semester to finish the series. You'll be here another couple years if you take those classes! I'm putting you in some fail-safe classes and you're graduating the end of this year!"

I looked down at the floor and my eyes stared at his black shoes. I felt cheated that I couldn't take what I wanted. I was dumped into another typing class, a homemaking class, and a marketing class. All we did was sit there and listen to lectures and you could pass just by showing up. I always made sure I showed up, but I don't know why. Part of me acted as if I wanted to graduate.

Meanwhile, I was still being punished for disobedience by being forced to see Miss Parker. Once a week, I had to listen to her tell me that I was a lesbian. My eyes burned from her cigarette smoke. Kids weren't allowed to smoke. Any kid caught smoking was suspended for a week. She would tell me about how she and her sister Helen spent their whole lives together. She would talk about their cottage and then she would talk about all the screwed up girls in our school.

"And you're screwed up too, Jill," she'd say as she pounded her fist on the desk, and the cigarette ashes spilled all over. "You're a lesbian. I just know it. You're a lesbian."

I was very confused about who I was and what I wanted in life. Her constant lecturing to me that I was a lesbian added to my confusion. She was an authority figure so I thought she must be right. I wasn't sure what a lesbian was, but I became convinced that I was one. I was convinced that there was something about me that told everyone that I was a lesbian. It was as if I had an invisible mark on me that I couldn't see, but everyone else could, especially Miss Parker.

One day I saw some posters on the school bulletin board. The posters were advertising the various school clubs. There were all kinds of clubs. To look at the posters, you got the impression that you had to be in a club or you were a non-existent non-thing. There was a tennis club and a drama club. There were sports clubs and art clubs and things I didn't know existed. But there was one club poster that popped out at me. It was from the biology club. The poster had drawings on it of bugs. Cute bugs. The meeting place and time fit right into my schedule, so I decided to attend. When I got there, I discovered there were only four members. All four were social outcasts. I fit right in. We talked about biology. We talked about life. We talked about how we all evolved from viruses, and that life was really a disease. We must have been the smallest club in school. There was no president or any other officers. I suggested that since there were only 5 of us, that each of us could have a title. They all agreed and I was immediately elected president. We even elected one guy as treasurer, even though we didn't collect dues or have a treasury. We met for about one hour a week. I was President of the school biology club and I had a D- average.

The school year ended and graduation day was coming. I

cried. I didn't want to graduate, yet I was about to, I did it to myself. I went to classes every day so I would pass. I don't know why.

The school photographer was coming to take individual photos of all the graduating seniors for the class year book. I didn't have money for a photo, so I asked my counselor if I could bring a photo from home.

"No," he said. "You find a way to pay like everyone else!"

My photo didn't get taken for the year book. I didn't have money to buy the class book anyway, so I figured it wasn't going to matter. But then, all the school clubs were sent notices to come to the photographer's station and get their group photo for the year book. The group photos were free! So there I was after all, listed as President of the school biology club.

Graduation was rapidly approaching, like a disease epidemic about to overtake me. Maurie gave me some money for my cap and gown. Such a wonderful, horrible brother. And then it happened. The disease struck. It was graduation day.

I never thought I'd live to see my own funeral. That's what that day seemed like. I stood under the bleachers watching the rain fall on the burial grounds. Graduation was only minutes away. The podium was being decorated for the presentation of the eulogy. Earlier in the morning, I had passed by my counselor's office on the way to my locker to get my belongings - the last of my remains. I waited till the last possible minute before giving up my locker forever. I pulled out all my books and notebooks, my ruler and pencil box, and a hair ribbon. I clutched my black parka jacket in my arms and looked into my emptied locker for the last time. My counselor saw me crying. He stepped out of his office, walked over to my locker, and smiled at me saying, "I knew you'd be happy about graduating." Then he turned around and stepped back into his office. After four years of high school, he still didn't understand. I don't cry when I'm happy.

My funeral was seconds away. The principal was standing at the podium, and pallbearers had placed a canopy over it. He was now ready to read the eulogy. Noisy crowds had gathered, but from somewhere in the back of my mind the sound of my mother's voice yelling at me overpowered it all. I heard her saying, "I can't wait till you're grown-up and out of the house. I can't wait till you die, Jill."

I opened the cardboard coffin that lay beside me, I put all my books and stuff from my locker into the box. Then I gently set my black parka into the coffin as if it were a dead baby. I took out the black death robe and put it on. I took off my tie shoes and placed them into the coffin as if to give my dead baby his favorite toys. I took out Johnny's moccasins and put them on my feet. I looked into the cardboard coffin. You weren't the freak, Johnny. It was Mother.

I looked down at my moccasins and wiggled my toes. I smiled under the tears. Wind blew into my robe and made the wings of my robe flap. I was a bird struggling to fly. I reached out for my diploma. I cried. It was now too late ever to be loved. No one would ever adopt me. My life was over.

Chapter 22 - Bye

Maurie had been among the crowd. He came up to me and took a picture of me in my cap and gown. Dad was at work. I wished he would have been there.

I went home. Miss Parker called to give me the name of the person whom I was supposed to see in her place. It was Miss Parker's job to refer kids elsewhere as soon as they graduated. She arranged for me to see Miss Harringdon at the Children's Center. The Children's Center was one of the agencies that had rejected me before, but now I would be going there again.

I walked into the familiar building of unfamiliar people. There was a new receptionist whom I hadn't seen before. I told her that I was there to see Miss Harringdon.

As far as the agency knew, I was just some new referral. I had assumed that Miss Parker had told them that I was there before, but she hadn't and no one ever asked me, so I didn't say anything.

Miss Harringdon was a tall, heavy-set woman. Her wrinkled face and gray hair made her look sixty, but her clothes and puffy teen-aged hair style made her look as if maybe she were in her twenties. She sat at her desk swinging her crossed leg, which drew attention to her bright red shoes. She sat with her arms folded, looked at her watch a lot, and hardly spoke to me. Each time I walked into her office, she would say, HI. I would say HI back. Then she sat silently waiting for me to speak and I waited for her to ask questions. Because she didn't ask, I didn't speak. Most of our sessions passed in silence. One time, she asked me what I was thinking. I asked her if she cared about me. She angrily yelled, "It doesn't matter what I think of you!"

I didn't want to talk to someone who didn't care. Weeks and months passed. We both sat on our chairs, while I gazed out the window and daydreamed. She sat with folded arms and swinging leg that from time to time would distract my daydreams.

While waiting for Miss Harringdon one day, I met another girl about my age who was also seeing Miss Harringdon. The other girl had given her the nickname of "cold fish." From that point on, I also referred to Miss Harringdon as the "cold fish."

I couldn't feel comfortable talking to the cold fish. Occasionally, when I did say something, she would say, "That's not related to your problem!" I didn't know what I was supposed to say, so I completely stopped talking, and daydreamed. One time she sneezed and it disrupted my daydream. I brought my eyes in from the window and looked up at her. "I forgot you were here," I told her. She looked at me as if she were staring at my invisible mark that announced that I'm a lesbian.

I hadn't been able to get into college because I had graduated from high school with a D- average. I was taking a special non-credit program at a local community college. It consisted of retaking basic high school courses to get into the regular curriculum. Having to take those classes made me feel even more inferior. I felt as if my invisible mark were attracting more attention. Having to retake dumb high school classes made me feel dumb. The registrar said that I had to take them to show if I had enough brains to do college work.. "Obviously, you can't be too bright or your high school grades would have been better," she said.

I continued living at home. I went to school every day and sat with Miss Harringdon for an hour, once a week. Occasionally, I would visit my high school biology teacher. My parents never asked me what I did all day and I never told them. I finished my semester of stupid classes and was admitted to the regular program at the community college. I was depressed because I believed that I would never get beyond a two-year college.

I fell apart. I became obsessed with memories of being tortured by Jacoby. It was like having a bad case of stomach flu. With the flu, you feel sick and throw up, and then you feel fine for awhile, and then you feel sick and need to throw up again. It was like that with my memories of Jacoby. Sometimes I could go to school and do whatever needed to be done. I felt O.K. But other times my obsession was so strong, my body could only pace the floor. My mind was imprisoned by Jacoby.

I didn't think about dating, sex, or marriage, like the other girls. I didn't want a husband. I wanted parents. I wanted to be someone's child. I assumed the reason that I didn't think about boys and marriage was because I was a lesbian. I remembered Miss Parker pounding her fist on her desk and telling me that I was a homosexual.

Memories of Jacoby were leeches draining me of my ability to think. I could no longer attend school. I would get up in the morning to go to school but somehow I would arrive so late that I would miss my class. I couldn't make it to school but I did keep my appointments with the cold fish, though I was often late. It was not unusual for me to walk in when there were only 15 minutes left of our one-hour appointment. I would go and sit but neither of us spoke. Then one day when I walked into her office, she unfolded her arms, stood up, and yelled at me, "I can't stand you anymore! Get out and don't come back!"

I looked up at her but said nothing. I left the office and wandered about the street for several hours. I decided to go to the Jewish Family Service - the other agency that had rejected me. Five or six years had passed since I had been there and I was hoping that the receptionist wouldn't recognize me. I walked in. There was a different receptionist. I asked to see someone and I was allowed to see Miss Kohler. Miss Kohler was a friendly, talkative lady with a German accent. She was smarter than the cold fish. One of the first things she did was to check records to see if I or anyone else in my family had ever been there. I wasn't going to volunteer such information even when asked because I was afraid that she would send me away because that was the order given by the previous social worker. So when Miss Kohler asked me if I had ever been there before, I didn't say anything. I hardly spoke anyway. But she was still friendly and smiled a lot. Because Miss Kohler checked the records she knew that I had been there and it took several sessions with her before I would admit to that. When she realized what the young incompetent social worker had done, she reported him. According to the notes in my case records, he had told his supervisor that he successfully placed my family and me in the hands of a psychologist at the Children's Center.

Miss Kohler was so angry with him that she rattled on for several minutes telling me that they were checking to see how many other people he had claimed to have referred away. Only then did I realize that he had done something wrong and it wasn't a matter of my not being worthwhile enough to be given help. I had, up until then, believed that the reason he sent me away was because I wasn't as important as those people he kept.

Miss Kohler said that she was leaving the agency soon for a better job that paid more money, and that there was no one competent in that agency. So she arranged for me to be seen at still another agency, Wayne County Mental Health Clinic. I saw a psychiatrist there 3 times a week for about 3 months, and then once a week for another 2 months. I felt like a limp rag doll. It was taking all my energies just to get to my appointments. Most days I paced around and thought about Jacoby.

"You're NOT a lesbian," the shrink kept telling me. "Everything you learned from your parents about marriage is wrong," he kept saying. "There is a reason why those girls at school were eager to grow up and get married. When people get married they are happy and they give affection to each other. Getting affection and love isn't something that disappears with age."

He somehow removed a barrier of fear to growing up. I stopped spending most of my time pacing around my bedroom. But the memory of Jacoby still burned my mind.

I remained in contact with my high school biology teacher. In fact, I had become his number one baby sitter.

"What's on your mind?" he probed. I told him that I was remembering again.

"You're hanging on to the torture, Jill. You're letting them continue to torture you. Push it out of your mind so they won't hurt you anymore."

I couldn't push it out of my mind. Mr. D knew that I had to get away from my mother, and he and his wife said that I could stay with them for a couple months until I could find somewhere else. My mind was that of a limp rag doll, I couldn't make decisions. It might take me all day to figure out what to eat for breakfast. With the help of the shrink, I finally made the decision that I would move, but I felt guilty. Johnny would be returning home. His status as ward of the court was over. I didn't want to leave him alone. I went with my parents to pick him up. Mom and Dad never asked him what he did up there.

Johnny and I unpacked his stuff. He tossed some clothes

into his closet and I picked up his pillow and clobbered him over the head. We played as if no time had ever separated us. "Johnny," I said, "my high school biology teacher said I could go live with him, but I feel sad because now you are finally home. I wish my teacher would let the two of us live with him, but he said he could only help me, and only for a few months."

Johnny smiled. "It's OK, Jill. I had my turn. Now you take yours." I hugged Johnny.

He said, "They tried to keep me longer at the boarding school, but they couldn't get the judge to extend his order. But, it will be OK, Jill. So, I finish high school at a public school. I'll be OK. You just take your turn."

I didn't want my parents to know I was moving out forever, so I told them I was going to spend a few days with a friend. Only Johnny knew what I was about to do. When no one noticed, I packed up all my things so I could make a quick move.

Mom and Dad were going to the grocery. "You kids want to come?" Mom called.

"No, not me," I answered.

"Yeah, I'll come," yelled Johnny and off they all went. I had bought a small pocket dictionary for Johnny and hid it in a shoe box. I placed it under his pillow and wrapped a note around it. I LOVE YOU, JOHNNY. LOVE JILL. On the inside cover I wrote down my new phone number, then quickly called my teacher. "They're gone," I told him. "You can come for me now."

All my stuff had been packed in boxes. I moved them to the front door so it would be easier and faster to get everything into the car. I ran back to my room for a last look to see if I had forgotten anything. My blanket. Winters are cold and I knew I would need my blanket. I grabbed it off my bed and was about to carry it to the rest of my stuff, but I stopped and put it back. I thought about Dad. It gets cold. Maybe he will need my blanket. I put my pink wool blanket back on my bed. The bed looked as if it were all set for me to sleep in. Mr. D drove up and in a moment we were both gone.

My shrink had been helpful, but unfortunately, he no longer wanted to see me after the 5 months. He was reducing his patient load and he announced that I was one of the people he decided not to continue with. On the last day that I saw him, he said,

"You'll be OK, now, but had I not helped you just when I did, you would have had a complete mental breakdown and that would have been the end for you. Had I not given you the emotional support to move away from home just when I did, your life would have been ruined. You were just weeks away from having your life destroyed. It would have been all over for you."

His words were piercing. I believed him.

Winter had set in and I was still with Mr. D's family. I was working part-time at a minimum- wage job in a department store and taking a class at the community college. It was all I could handle. I was only making enough money to pay tuition and have bus fare back and forth. I never ate lunch; no money. I wish I could have continued to see another shrink, but the clinic only would allow me to see more incompetent people. They were all young and many didn't even have degrees.

At Christmas, a classmate had given me a stuffed elf. I was happy and decided to show it to Miss R., the counselor that I had been assigned to. Miss R. had red hair and red nail polish. She was young and had just graduated from college.

On the wall, behind her chair, was a calendar with pictures of sailboats. She told me that she loved sailboats and loved to go to boat races and pretend that all the boats were hers.

When I showed her my elf, she said, "Well, is it a good elf or a bad elf?" I laughed.

"I'm serious!" she said. "You only brought it in because it has a special fantasy for you. Now what is the fantasy?"

"I was just happy that a classmate liked me well enough to give me something."

"Nonsense. This is therapy," she said as she stretched out her fingers admiring her red polish. "You wouldn't bring something in unless it had great psychological fantasies for you."

I wanted to tell her about school and talk about my future. I liked being in college, but I was also afraid of graduating because it would make me too adult. I told her I wanted to talk about school, but before I could finish my sentence she said, "Come now, I know you have fantasies about the elf. What are they?"

I sat in silence. She wouldn't allow me to talk about the things I wanted and I became depressed. No agency that I ever tried since has assigned me to anyone who helped.

Whenever I talked to Johnny, he said that everything was fine. Then a neighbor called me. "Can't you do something?" she said. "Your mother threw your brother and father out of the house and they had to sleep in the car all night in this freezing cold!"

I was silent. Why didn't the neighbor invite them into her house? I wondered.

"My mother always does those things," I finally replied. "I don't know what to do."

Spring arrived. I was still at my teacher's and not doing well enough to move out yet. It was hard enough to hold down a part-time job, and in order for me to have enough money to pay rent anywhere, I would need a full-time job. As it was, I was hungry. I went from my part-time job to school, and came back at the end of the day without ever eating.

I called my father at work and arranged to meet him at a nearby shopping center. It was on his way home anyway. He smiled when he saw me. I could tell he was glad to see me.

"Dad," I said, "can you give me some money for lunches?"

"Mom is acting up," he said, and his smile crumbled into sadness. "If you want food, you can move back home! You left me alone with her! I can't handle her by myself."

"I can't come back home, Dad."

"You left me, Jill. How am I supposed to handle Mom?"

He looked as if he were about to cry.

"Maybe you could just give me some money for bread and peanut butter."

"I don't have extra money, Jill. Mom is costing me all I have on those mental hospitals."

"OK, Dad. You don't need to give me anything. I'm old enough to take care of myself."

I looked down at my boots. They had holes in them and the rain crept in.

"Dad," I said, "I worry about Johnny. Maybe you can help him."

"I'm going to be planting more radishes this year," he answered. "You should see my garden, Jill."

By summer, I finally got a job at a summer camp and had arranged to stay with a classmate in the fall. I continued to work part-time and attend class. I was always hungry.

Johnny graduated from high school and went away to a community college with the help of a welfare program. The school was in a different city. He was safe from Mom.

Years were passing. I was in and out of minimum-wage

jobs. Minimum-wage was all that I was ever offered. It was the 1960's, and girls rarely were given good jobs. The boring, minimum-wage jobs made me feel worthless. Humans were not my peers. I was something less. I stood all day in department stores and sold clothes to others that I could never afford for myself. My feet hurt, I shifted my weight from one foot to the other, and kept thinking about food. I felt weak. I had headaches. My salary wasn't enough for food and rent. The other sales girls were also students but they had families who were supporting them. Their salaries went for clothes and sorority dues. I lived in the cheapest rooms I could find. I paid rent and tuition for a class, and what little was left went for something to eat. At night I dreamt about food.

Hope did not exist. I was a condemned prisoner with a life sentence. I had only my daily schedule of work and school and that would continue till death. It took much strength to get out of bed in the morning. Wasting my life at boring jobs, made me feel as if I were a prisoner locked in a coffin waiting to die. One of my jobs was to make "X"s in a little square in the corner of sales slips. Each morning, one of the workmen would wheel in to my desk, a large box, the size of a trash can. It was full of sales slips. My job was to take one out at a time, put an "X" on it, and put it into another box. Hour after hour, I made "X"s. By the end of the day, my head hurt. At night I dreamt about the letter "X". Such jobs should be the punishment for real prisoners.

Only for brief segments of time was I allowed out of my coffin and the freedom of attending a class. School was my escape from boredom and depression. It was an oasis where I had friendly classmates. I could be with my own species. The classes I liked best were psychology and physics, and so those were the classes I kept taking. I wanted to understand people and what made them the way they were. I wanted to understand the origins of people, planets, and the forces of the universe. Psychology explained the people, and physics explained the universe in which they lived

Five years passed and somehow I had finished enough credits to complete my 2-year college. I applied to the local university and continued on. So now I was in a university instead of a community college, but I was still condemned to a life sentence of boring jobs.

I never applied for a student loan because I was sure I would never graduate and be able to pay it back. Eventually, however, I was offered a scholarship with a generous stipend. I no longer had to work. At that point I was able to go to school full-time and even overload my schedule. I had been in college for a total of eight years, when my advisor informed me that I had enough credits for a degree. I hadn't been counting. I never thought I'd reach that point.

Unlike my high school graduation, this time I was happy. I got together with classmates and celebrated. One of my classmates was Rob, a tall, thin guy with messy hair, who looked like a comedian. He was a class clown. When he wanted to, he had a way of walking and looking at you that made everyone laugh, yet he wrote serious political essays. He had strong feelings about political issues, and he wanted to be a writer. He and I and several others partied all night after graduation. We dined on cake, ice cream, and hot dogs. We acted like small children at a birthday party. I was happy, but embarrassed that my four-year degree took eight years. I told everyone except Rob and a couple other close friends that I was four years younger than I really was.

I applied for several jobs that were listed in the university career center. Employers came to campus to interview prospective students. IBM was interested in me, and they asked me to take a series of tests. I passed with superior grades on all of them and IBM asked me to go to New York to work for them as a computer programmer trainee. They said they would pay all my moving expenses. And, the salary was much higher than any other company was offering. I declined the offer. I didn't think it was fair to waste their money for a job that would only last a few weeks before I was fired. I had been fired from all my previous jobs, so I was sure this one would be the same. Jobs were boring and made me so depressed and gave me such bad headaches that I could not function well. If I could keep a job for an entire school term, I felt I was lucky. A woman from IBM called me and asked me to reconsider my decision. She said I had an unusually high aptitude. I said, "No." Aptitude meant nothing. I'm sure my aptitude for putting Xs on sales slips, or my aptitude for standing on my feet in a department store as a sales clerk, was high too. High aptitude never stopped me from getting fired. So, I said, "No." Instead, I looked for a job in Detroit. Rob was also looking for a job. He searched the want ads everyday. "Look," he said, showing me the newspaper. "There doesn't seem to be many jobs, yet there are job openings in employment agencies." A mischievous grin covered his face.

A few days later, he called me. He said he had gotten a job in an employment agency and his goal was to get jobs for all his friends, and ignore all the clients that were being assigned to him.

"But, if you ignore the clients assigned to you, you will be fired!" I yelled at him through the phone.

"Yep. That's the idea," he said. "Then I can collect unemployment and have time for my writing. I just spent my first day looking for a job for you. I found a chemical company that needs lab help. You like science. Go get it!"

I went. I got the job. It paid a livable wage and didn't bore me into deep depression. I actually liked the job. I kept wondering when they were going to fire me. One day the director came into the lab. My body stiffened. I knew I was about to be fired. In an angry voice he said, "Do any of you know where Howard's lab report is?"

"No," We replied. He walked back out. Every time the director came into the lab, I thought for sure it was because he was about to fire me. But his reasons for coming into the lab were never to tell me that I had lost the job.

Rob managed to make his employer think that he was trying to help clients, but he was just too incompetent to do the job. So Rob got laid off and got his unemployment. After one year, I quit my job. It was the first job that I ever left by choice.

*

I moved to San Francisco, Sun Funcisco, as I called it. I knew the state of California was the land for sun-hugged youth. It was the land of young people from all over the country, enveloped in sunshine. I was not going to tolerate another Michigan winter. I checked myself into the YWCA and began a new life. My first job was in a paint lab. It was smelly, and paint pigments floated through the air. It was hard to breathe in there. I hated it.

In order to save as much money as possible I moved into a one-bedroom apartment with 6 other girls. I had met one of them at the bus stop. She took the same bus I did everyday to go to work. But she worked in a fabric store. Through her I met the rest of her roommates. One of them would be moving out in a few months, but I was welcome to join them now if I wanted. They belonged to a religious cult and believed they could tell their god what to do. In their nightly prayers, I would hear them say, "Our friend Sara needs to know if she should marry Bert. She needs to know by noon tomorrow when they meet for lunch. So be sure to give her a sign. And Maryanne just broke up with Gary, so she needs a new boyfriend. Be sure he is good-looking this time."

But the thing we had in common was that we all wanted to save money. They all slept on mats in the bedroom. There wasn't room for me in there too, so I slept in the living room. We ate together and lived like a rat pack of sorority sisters.

I kept working at the paint lab, and looking for other jobs. One year later, I found work in an international engineering firm, as a computer operator. There were engineers from around the world, but mainly from the Middle East and Far East. It was a time when those areas felt they needed nuclear power plants. But in those places, supervisors often took bribes to say that things were safe when they weren't. So the governments protected themselves by contracting the work through American supervision. I became friends with these engineers. On weekends, we often had parties and they taught me how to cook their food, and even taught me to speak some of their languages. I loved "speaking in tongues." They told me about their extended families back home. They told me that if I ever wanted to travel, they would arrange for me to stay with their families. They even had special, slightly corrupt travel agents who could help me travel cheaply. I could not resist their offers.

I traveled to the Middle East and lived in Iran. I stood at the ancient ruins where Darius had once stood. It was as if I had fallen into a black hole and arrived in another universe. I was in a world where time had stopped two thousand years ago. Women washed their clothes in the streams. Shepherds roamed the desert with their sheep.

I had dark eyes and dark hair and was living with an Iranian family. Everyone assumed I was an uneducated village girl who had come to live with rich relatives in the city. No one, outside of my host family, believed me when I said I was American. No American girl would come by herself to a Moslem country. People made fun of me for trying to pretend to be American. I would say things to my host family that they didn't believe either. I would say, "In the U.S., people put their garbage in the sink. And it goes down the same hole where the water goes."

They laughed. My host father would say, "What a wild imagination she has!"

People were either rich or poor. I lived among the rich. My U.S. dollars were going a long way. In this part of the universe, I had become transformed into a Persian princess. The poor reminded me of my life in Detroit, when I lived from day to day with no hope. I saw young children working as servants, and orphaned children surviving by being slaves in the homes of the rich. The goal of these children was to stay alive. Status was surviving.

The Shah was in power. The U.S. had a large military base there and were keeping the Shah in power. The people hated the Shah, but the U.S. needed the Shah, and the military base, and the oil. The American newspapers said that the Shah was modernizing the country. But everyone in the country knew that the only thing he was modernizing was the wardrobe of the Queen. In spite of American efforts to keep the Shah in power, the people were willing to fight to their death to get rid of him. The revolutionary movement was getting stronger. I spent a year in Iran, and then had to flee.

I went to Vancouver, Canada. Canada because they have national health insurance, and I wanted to be somewhere, where if anything happened to me while I was between jobs, I would be protected. I chose Vancouver because the weather is mild. Canada would not let me have a landed immigrant status. They said they had too many Americans flocking to Canada. Americans were coming up to avoid the military draft, and to avoid the forced bussing taking place in American schools.

My money was getting low, and I knew I would have to cross the border and get a job quickly. The nearest large American city was Seattle. I got on a train, and went. It was now summer, there were a lot of cheap rooms for rent in the University of Washington area, and jobs around campus were easy to find. I also secured a teaching assistant job for the fall. I would be in school - again.

*

Memories of Jacoby and my mother were napalmed to my mind. I remembered her telling me not to tell anyone what we did at his office all day. Now I was determined to tell everyone. Every chance I got I would write letters to my mother's psychiatrists or social workers. I wanted everyone to know, and I wanted to find out who Jacoby was and how my mother met him. I wrote letters to the Wayne County Medical Association, but they had no record of him. I wrote to the owners of the Fisher Building where he worked, but they never answered. I wrote to the newspapers, but no one helped me. I even went to a minister who wrote letters for me to my mother telling her it is wrong to torture small children. Whenever I talked to my father on the phone, he asked, "How come you write such letters?" The tone of his voice told me he was confused. He said it couldn't be true because mothers don't do "such things." He never said what those "such things" were. We talked about my "such letters" and the "such things" as if we were speaking a secret code. In my very last conversation with him, I said, "NORMAL mothers don't do those "such things." Is she NORMAL, Dad?" There was silence. "Dad?" I yelled out breaking the quietness. "Well, Dad? Look at her. Is she normal?"

"No," he answered. Then, slowly the words fell out of his mouth and through the phone, "She's not normal." It was as if he was finally waking up from his sleep-walking dream. I was surprised. I was almost sure he was going to say that there was nothing wrong with Mom, and he would be planting radishes. I had never heard him say before that she wasn't normal.

"Jill, I feel sick."

I could hear he was having trouble catching his breath.

"I'd like to see you, Jill."

"I never want to come back!" I shouted.

"Are you happy in Seattle?" he asked.

"Yes, Dad, and I never want to come back home."

"Jill, you're in your 30's now. How come you're not married? I'd like to see you married."

"Dad! You'll never see that day!"

He cried, and he hung up.

My mother had always wanted me to get married so I would be out of her house. Marriage meant the ultimate rejection by a parent. When Dad asked me about marriage, I exploded in rage. If I ever did get married, I wouldn't even want to tell him. If he couldn't be my father when I was a child, then I didn't want him after I was grown up. That was the last time I spoke to him.

I continued writing letters, and I also called the house in the middle of the night. As soon as I heard the phone pick up, I hung up. A mother who tortures her baby doesn't deserve to sleep. I asked the minister to continue writing letters for me also. When I told him that I was calling in the middle of the night, he said, "But you're waking your father, too."

"I don't care," I replied.

"What if they kill each other?" he asked.

"I don't care." I said. "If my father gets angry enough and kills her, then he will finally be free of her. Maybe then, he can finally get help."

The Minister refused to write more letters.

Night after night, I continued to call the house. No one knew it was me. Between my letters and my midnight phone calls, I was going to get back at her.

Johnny told me later that Dad was sick with high blood pressure. He was supposed to take medication and get rest. Mom kept throwing his medicine away. She became violent and smashed furniture, dishes and anything else that got in her way.

In my burning rage, I forgot that Dad was all alone with Mom . Mom had been the youngest of 7 children, and now there was only one sibling left. The rest were dead. When we were young, the relatives came because for them it was a party. But at least having others around was moral support for Dad. Now there was no one. Her one remaining brother no longer wanted to come. I called every night and forgot that without other people around, Dad wouldn't be able to even go out for food.

I was to find out later that he had called the police for help, because Mom, in her violence, beat him up. He was bruised and bleeding from a knife wound. But the police wouldn't do anything. A woman who gets beat up can be taken to a battered woman's shelter. There was no place for Dad, and the police wouldn't take Mom. Dad was never able to call the police before. Dad handled everything alone this time. He committed Mom a couple of times but she signed herself out. Then, finally, he had arranged for legal papers to be drawn up for a longer commitment. He only needed to push Mom into the car and pick up the papers then drive on to the hospital.

The next morning he got her into the car and drove to pick up the papers. People on the street watched as Mom beat him with her fists. He passed out. Mom grabbed the steering wheel and steered the car into a parked car. Dad was dead. Witnesses called the police and Mom was finally taken away.

I flew in for the funeral. Johnny took me to the house for one last time. I looked at Dad's garden. His radishes and tomatoes would soon die without him. No one would be watering the plants and the grass would grow tall and bury everything.

Inside the house, the refrigerator was taped up with thick wrapping tape, the kind you use to send packages far away. A note from Maurie was taped to the handle. It said, "Do not touch my mother's food. I'm getting her out of the hospital. There's nothing wrong with her. She's coming back."

Chapter 23 - End

"Where's the scissors, Johnny? I'm cutting the damn tape! Maurie is really a jerk!"

"No, Jill. Leave it alone. I'd rather not bother with Maurie. Let him be a jerk."

I looked around the house. Aside from the refrigerator, everything looked normal. Some dishes were soaking in the sink. The floors had been swept and the carpets vacuumed. Dad's favorite chair was pulled up to the T.V., as if he were about to return.

We went back to Johnny's place to eat. I opened Johnny's refrigerator. It was full of food, mainly hot dogs, pies, and ice cream.

"Don't you eat fruits or vegetables?" I asked.

"Sure," he said. "I eat cherry, apple, and banana pies, strawberry ice cream, and frozen pizza with veggies on it."

Johnny broiled a bunch of hot dogs while I wandered around. I pretended not to noticed girl's tights in his room.

After stuffing ourselves with hot dogs, we went to the mental hospital to talk to Mom's doctor. We walked through a ward where a group of staring patients stood, scattered around the room. I stared at all the faces as they stared at me. I felt like a mouse that had wandered into a lions' cage.

Johnny walked several steps ahead of me. "Come on, Jill."

I dashed forward to catch up to him. A nurse sitting behind a desk told us which way to go to see Mom's doctor. He was a friendly man, about 40 years old, who smiled when he saw us.

"Your mother should never be released, but unfortunately the law doesn't allow us to keep her indefinitely. It will be up to you, the children, to put her in a halfway house or nursing home where they keep such people." He gave us a list of places to check out and told us that she could be legally put in one of those places, but not in a hospital.

"You'll have to decide which place is best for her, " he said. Your older brother doesn't understand her condition, so you may have a court battle with him, but your Mom should not be sent back home."

It seemed too late in my life to stay and fight out a court battle with Maurie. Locking her up after the damage was done seemed ironic. I had more important things to do than fight with Maurie.

As Johnny and I left, we passed by the recreation room where Mom and several other patients were. Mom was lying on the ping pong table. Her hair looked as if a circus monkey had combed it for her. Her eyes stared at us. Johnny stood there for a moment looking at her.

"Come on, Johnny. Let's go," I said.

Johnny just stood there. I looked at Mom. In some way, it was as if I were looking into a mirror. It wasn't that I looked like her. It was because I was part of her. I remembered the psychiatrist at the Wayne County Mental Health Clinic. I had only seen him for a few months. He said that I was only a few weeks away from having my life totally destroyed. I don't know if he was right or not, but the thought of ending up like my mother terrified me.

Mom loved being crazy. It was a game to control others. Ironically, the game controlled her. I walked towards the door and looked back at her. She was looking around the room at the other patients who couldn't play ping pong because she controlled the table. She smiled as if enjoying her power. My mother was a true praying mantis. She got rid of her mate, and was in complete control. I looked back at her for the last time. I walked away. I was lucky.

As Johnny and I arrived at the airport, I thought about

Maurie and Mom's refrigerator. I pictured my father in his garden with his radishes. My mother's laughter echoed in my mind. I kissed Johnny good bye. Perhaps having him to love is what helped me survive. I got on the plane to return to grad school at the University of Washington. I wondered what would happen to Johnny. I remembered the pair of tights I saw in his apartment. I remembered the words of Uncle Frank. "You stick to your older brother, Jill. Someday your younger brother will grow up and move away."

I fastened my seat belt. "No, Uncle Frank," I mumbled. "It is I who moved away."

The plane moved. I left for the last time.

EPILOGUE

I remember the image of someone I knew. We were young then. She must have been about 13. I was a little older. She was wearing a black parka. I will always remember that black parka. I found her lying on the floor, unconscious. She was wearing that black parka. I stood over her. I wanted to save her but I didn't know how. If one of us had to die, I wanted it to be me. I was older and had less to live for. I didn't want her to die. I loved her. I didn't want her to die so much, that even today, I have not yet accepted the fact that I couldn't save her. I took off her shoes and I wore them. I wore her shoes and her clothes. The kids at school knew I was wearing her clothes and her shoes, and they told me how dumb I looked wearing her things because they didn't fit me right. They looked good on her but not me. I was too old to wear her style clothes. But I didn't care. I continued to wear her things. I wasn't going to let her die. I think somewhere in my boxes of storage, I still have that black parka. I hung on to her by wearing her clothes. I wasn't going to let her die. She became part of me. She was me. She continued to live through me. I haven't let her die. She didn't really die at all. She's the childhood I kept alive. I have watched her many times lying on the floor hidden in the crevices of my mind. She's my dying childhood. Her clothes, those clothes I used to wear to school. They were my own.

The End

My Last Remains

My Last Remains

Denlinger's Publishers, Ltd., "The InstaBook publisher for tomorrow's great authors... today!", hopes you have enjoyed reading this book.

We will forward your emailed comments to the author upon request. [support@thebookden.com].

Visit our on-line bookstore for additional **InstaBook** titles, electronic book titles (**eBooks**), and both **GemStar** edition titles, formerly known as Rocket eBook and SoftBook.

http://www.thebookden.com

This book was produced by **InstaBook** system technology.

Mission Statement

We will earnestly strive to enrich and entertain our customers through reading by promoting one of our constitutional rights, "freedom of speech." And, with honesty and integrity, strive to recognize and promote authors by publishing their works.

Denlinger's Publishers & Bookstore

P.O. Box 1030 – Edgewater, FL 32132-1030

My Last Remains